STATUE IN THE MOONLIGHT

M. BONNEAU

CONTENTS

AUTHOR'S NOTE

This book is for all the reckless adventurous young women in the world. I hope we can all see ourselves represented in romance novels, enjoying a well-deserved happily ever after. It's true what we say: "well behaved women rarely make history." They rarely have fun, either. Let's raise a glass to following our dreams, being who we want to be no matter what anyone says, and never forgetting to have fun!

Many thanks to my parents for paying for a state-of-the-art Creative Writing degree for me, and then not freaking out when I chose to use that degree by writing romances. Mom and dad, you're my best cheerleaders.

And thank you, readers, for welcoming my characters into your libraries. They'd be homeless if not for you!

~M.

CHAPTER ONE

The evening had passed well beyond tediousness for Anthony Maltravers, Viscount Stirling, first son of the Earl of Huntington. He had arrived at Lady Spencer's ball no less than an hour late in an attempt to shorten the time between his arrival and his planned assignation with a certain honorable (soon to be dis-honorable) Miss, who had only arrived in town the week before. However, when he'd entered the ballroom and caught the young lady's eye, she had beat a hasty retreat to her parents and feigned a headache, and for the past two hours he had been unable to escape the dullness of social obligations and head for home, a hot bath, and perhaps a low woman to relieve his frustration. He sighed. The virgins of Bath were becoming easier to seduce and harder to bed. And as for the matrons and widows of society... well, they were easy to bed and required no seduction at all. The finesse and talent of the studied rake, he mused as he downed his sixth glass of wine and summoned a footman to pour him a seventh, was no longer appreciated in England.

On the dance floor couples were gathering for the third waltz. His brain unable to take any more spinning than was absolutely necessary, Anthony headed for the card room. Halfway through the door, however, he was spotted by the widow Walters, his too-willing conquest of last month. She bowed her head in acknowledgement and flicked her tongue over her lower lip. He shuddered involuntarily at the thought of having to put up with her mewling, childish cries of ecstasy for another night. Bowing his head curtly, he headed for the host's library.

He closed the door behind him, inhaling the scent of leather and dusty paper. Ah, books! How he had detested them as a youth! He avoided opening them even now. But the beautiful thing about the libraries of Bath was that everyone left them, and their dull residents, alone. Libraries were custom made for solitude during mind-numbing social events, as well as the occasional assignation.

A breeze from the library's open bay windows swept through the room, relieving some of the stale odor. Fresh air. Pushing his deceptively cherubic blond curls away from his sweating forehead and setting his wine glass on a table, Anthony moved to the balcony to clear his head.

He stood in the doorway a moment, eyes adjusting to the darkness of the night sky, before he noticed that he was not alone. At the far end of the balcony a figure stood, leaning out over the railing, satin gloved hands gripping the balustrade. For a moment he thought the woman must be a statue: she was standing so still, the pale skin of her arms and neck shining like marble in the moonlight. Then the breeze stirred across the balcony again, fluttering her dress ever so slightly and making her shiver. Not a member of the resident garden statuary, then.

He stepped closer to see what she was looking at in the gardens below but was surprised to see that her eyes were closed, her chin tucked into her chest and her lips pulled thin in a... grimace? Her delicate silk dress glowed deep purple where the moon shone on it, and black in the darkness where it did not, sharply contrasting with the pale freckled skin of her face and chest, and for a moment he thought she must be something inhuman. A Greek Fate? A fairy queen, perhaps?

Her chest expanded in a deep breath, the scandalous crease of shadow between her breasts catching his attention. He allowed himself another moment of silence to inspect her. Her appearance was unusual to say the least. She wore her hair, which appeared red in the moonlight, in a severe chignon, allowing only one curl to escape and cascade down the side of her neck. The simple style was decidedly unfashionable, however it served to highlight her high cheekbones and strong jawline to perfection, enhancing his earlier idea that she was, indeed, a symmetrically carved statue. Her dress was cut low on her chest, and she had left the expanse of skin between her neck and breasts free of jewels, which puzzled him, as the dress and gloves she wore were obviously some of the finest and most expensive available in Bath. Her bosom, he noted with appreciation, was large for her lean frame, and sloped down to an almost boyish waist and hips, revealed by the cling of her gown in the night breeze.

Lust.

The emotion surged to mind as he drank in her form. No, he could not group her with the other women in his life who had inspired lust: the curvaceous, delicate, fashionably styled women. It was something more like... need for this statuesque creature who was somewhere between woman and

Goddess. Need to caress her skin and convince himself that it was not the cold, polished stone it appeared to be. Need to kiss the pursed lips, feel them open and swell under his own. Need to run his thumbs along her cheekbones as he cupped her face in his hands, a welcoming smile blossoming under his touch. And perhaps, he conceded, as the shallowness of his breathing called him back from his fantasies, just a hint of lust.

He could have her, now. In three steps he could have his arms around her waist, press his lips against hers before she could cry out. He could hold her in his embrace until he was sure she would make no protest to his advances, feel her stiffness and poise melt under his expert touch. He took those three silent steps to close the distance between them, standing behind her so closely he could feel the heat of her body through her thin gown. She was most certainly not cold marble.

She seemed to sense his presence, lifting her chin but keeping her eyes closed. He reached out a fingertip to trace the line of her collarbone, and wrapped the other arm around her ribs just below her breasts. She didn't shrink from his presumptuous caress, didn't speak. Emboldened, Anthony pressed her back against himself. The firm round contour of her buttocks against his thighs was almost too exquisite, and his growing erection pushed into her lower back. She felt it and began to pull away, a grimace at the corners of her mouth, and the frown of disgust on her face stopped him from kissing her just long enough for her to speak.

"Not here," she said, her voice deep and ragged like torn velvet, the statement halfway between begging and demanding. Ignoring her, he brushed his lips along her neck where the single tendril of soft hair had absconded from her chignon. The curl tickled his lips. He chuckled against her skin. She smelled of sandalwood soap, a mild, earthy, almost masculine scent. The woman did not pull away, but she turned her face away from him, lowering her chin into her chest again as if to insulate herself from his warmth. She spoke barely above a whisper, the edge of disdain in her voice sharp enough to wound him where the words struck: "I see town has taught you some tenderness."

His lips stopped their ministrations and he released his arms from around her waist ever so slightly. The tone in her voice was clear. She thought he was someone else. She had allowed him to touch her only because she was expecting a rendezvous with another man. A man who was evidently not tender. He cleared his throat. "Madam, tenderness has always been a part of my reputation."

She opened her eyes in surprise at the unfamiliar sound of his voice and looked over her shoulder at him. He watched her eyes, black as her dress in the darkness, assess every inch of his face before settling on his lips, her expression warring between surprise and relief and perhaps even... hope?

She turned slowly to face him and brought one gloved hand up to his mouth, allowing his shallow breath to fall on her fingertips for a moment. He thought he saw the beginning of a devilish smile twitch at the corners of her lips, but the next moment she had pressed herself against him and brought her mouth up to his, her kiss so violent and desperate his teeth ached against hers. She gripped his shoulder with one hand and snaked the other behind his head, spreading her satin covered fingers through his hair. Anthony pulled her hips into him, forcing her belly against the throbbing need in his breeches. Through the thin material of her dress, he thought he could feel a tremor of pleasure pass quickly up her side as she exhaled a small sigh into his mouth. She released the kiss for a moment, then caught his lower lip between her teeth.

She bit down and he gasped, kneading her backside with one hand as the other sought her breasts.

Then she pushed him away and the moment was gone as quickly as it had begun. He staggered back and opened his eyes. She, too, was gone, the curtains at the library windows rustling after her as she ran away.

Licking his tongue over his lower lip, he tasted blood. *Good God*, was the only thought he could muster. What *was* that? What was *she*?

CHAPTER TWO

"Have I got a story for you, Darling!" Anthony exclaimed as he sank into a chair at his gentlemen's club. His friend, Quincy Darling, stirred from what was obviously a nasty hangover and gave Anthony a bilious look. "Come, come, man. Wake up," Anthony insisted, handing the man a glass of brandy. "I'm in need of your advice."

Darling pushed himself up in his chair and accepted the alcohol, downing it in one gulp. "Stirling, you ass," he said. "What time is it?"

"It's nearing noon," Anthony answered impatiently.

His friend closed his eyes with a petulant snort. "Then it is nearly three hours too early for you to be speaking to me."

Anthony continued, unfazed. "I've met a woman."

"Nothing new," Darling answered.

"I don't know who she is and I need your inestimable social knowledge to ferret her out." Anthony pushed his own glass of brandy into his friend's hand. "Wake up, help me figure out who she is, and then I'll let you sleep it off."

"I don't see what's so damned urgent about it," Darling growled.

Anthony paused for a moment, then he said the one detail of interest in his story that could possibly rouse his friend. "She bit me."

Darling opened his eyes. "She what?" he exclaimed.

"She bit me. Here." Anthony pulled his lower lip down with his forefinger to reveal the minute teeth marks inside it.

His friend squinted at the swollen lip and chuckled. "She bit you and you don't even know her name?"

"Our acquaintance was… brief." Anthony raised an eyebrow tellingly.

"Very well." Darling made a show of sighing, but the twinkle in his eyes belied his interest. "You've sufficiently intrigued me. Describe your vixen."

"Well," Anthony began, "She is tall, up to here." He motioned to his nose, and his friend raised his eyebrows in surprise, as the height Anthony had indicated was unusually tall for a woman. "Titian hair, simply styled. Pale skin. Some freckles. Generous bosom. The rest of her is lean though, almost unfeminine. Except for her backside," he added with a sly grin, "which is magnificently feminine."

"And where did you meet this mysterious Amazon?" Darling asked.

"Lady Spencer's ball last night."

"Sadly, I was not in attendance," Darling said. "A certain young widow required my comforting presence."

Anthony ignored him. "But do you know anyone of that description?"

"I should say not," Darling frowned. "She certainly sounds like a striking presence, not someone I would easily forget. You should have got her name, Stirling. That was damn foolish of you."

Anthony grimaced. How could he explain to an equally notorious rake that this woman had rendered him incapable of speech? Incapable, for a few seconds of pure bliss, of anything other than reveling in the kiss she'd given him?

No woman had ever taken his breath away before. He prided himself on keeping his head in the bedroom. Perhaps it was the wine, not her. Perhaps in that state of intoxication any woman would have rendered him helpless. But he knew that was a lie. He'd bedded woman before with much more than six glasses of wine in him and he'd maintained control over his thoughts and actions. It was something about this woman in particular that had made him feel momentarily like one of his own conquests. *And you liked it, you little traitor*, he told his heart as it raced at the memory of her body pressed against his. *I always knew I couldn't trust you.*

"Stirling? Anthony?" his friend's words shook him out of his reverie. "What are your intentions for your little biter?"

What were his intentions? To seduce her the way she had seduced him, so quickly and completely. To toss her onto a bed and tear off her dress. Make her melt under his caresses as she had failed to do on the library balcony. Bury his face between her breasts, and his cock between her legs. To make her senseless with a desire that would eclipse the desire he felt for her. And to make her taste the fulfillment and satisfaction she had denied him when she ran from him last night, whether she wanted it or not. To claim back his initiative from her, make him the conqueror again. Make sure she knew that the pleasurable torture she'd inflicted on him he could give her back again tenfold.

He flashed a wicked smile at Darling. "I'm sure you can guess."

Darling chuckled. "Well, I hope for the poor vixen's sake you don't find her, then. But if you do have your mind set on her, why not try the Renfield salon this evening, or Harrington's ball in two days? If she was invited to Lady Spencer's, she'll certainly be in attendance there. And then you can exact your revenge. Though," he said, and his eyes twinkled with aggressive mirth, "based upon your previous encounter, she might enjoy whatever debauches you have planned for her."

"I hope she does, Darling," Anthony replied, "or it will be a decidedly unpleasant evening for her."

CHAPTER THREE

Anthony had not planned to attend Lady Renfield's salon. He abjured the intellectual evenings of new music and art and witty repartee. The skill of his tongue had never lain in conversation, but in the bedroom, and his appreciation of art was limited to the various proportions of the female form. However, he penned a hasty acceptance letter to Lady Renfield, countering his earlier polite refusal with profuse apologies.

Though he arrived at the salon late enough to miss the first musical sojourn and just in time for dinner, his Amazon, as Darling had aptly named her, was not in attendance. He concealed his disappointment with a few glasses of port after the meal, and forced himself to stay through the rest of the evening. Lady Renfield was a doting hostess, introducing him to every intellectual gentleman in the room, marveling that

Viscount Stirling himself, scion of the ancient and noble Huntington line, had deigned to attend his *first* Bath salon at *her* house. He endured a few good natured jabs from the *beau monde* in attendance about giving up his hedonistic life in the pursuit of art, and returned home ill-tempered and slightly sloshed, releasing his frustration on his valet as the poor man helped him undress. Sleep came as an unwelcome and cold bedfellow, and he wished as he drifted into dreams that he'd ordered his carriage driver to take him to a brothel instead of his own lonely house.

A breeze from the library's open bay windows swept through the room, relieving some of the stale odor. Fresh air. He set his wine glass on a table and moved to the balcony to clear his head. He stood in the doorway a moment, eyes adjusting to the darkness of the night sky, before he noticed that he was not alone. At the far end of the balcony, a statue stood: pale and cold marble in the moonlight. A thin Grecian dress trembled against the stone in the nocturnal draft, and he watched as it clung to the pert breasts, round buttocks, long poised legs. He reached out, caressed the figure's arm, traced the finely carved strands of hair flowing languidly down its back. He kissed the hard neck, cupped the unforgiving breasts. The statue stirred, tendrils of warmth and plush skin weaving their way across its surface. It turned to him, its engraved eyes whispering possessive intent into his soul. He kissed it, the stone mouth warming under his lips. It kissed back, catching his lower lip between its granite flavored teeth and biting down. He tasted blood --

The pain woke Anthony with a start. Morning's light was

barely stealing through the bed curtains. He gingerly touched his mouth where his own teeth had closed over his lip, reopening the small wounds his mysterious lady had given him on the library balcony. Wincing, he rang the servants' bell and ordered his butler to bring him a cold compress.

Chapter Four

"Champagne at ten in the morning? How gauche," Anthony admonished as he took a seat beside Darling in their club. His friend looked up from the morning paper in surprise.

"Hair of the dog, dear boy. Nothing better than champagne. And good morning to you as well. Didn't think I'd be seeing you today. Thought you'd have a certain toothy Amazon's legs still wrapped around your waist," Darling answered, chuckling. "I take it you had no success at Renfield's."

Anthony grunted. "She wasn't there."

Darling took an appreciative sip of champagne and smiled amusedly at his friend. "Now, don't you sound petulant."

"You would know; you always sound petulant," Anthony laughed.

"I do not!" The pages of Darling's newspaper fluttered as he tossed it aside in gentlemanly outrage.

"Aha!" Anthony exclaimed, pointing. "You see?"

The dandy began to roll his eyes, but then apparently realized how truly petulant that looked and settled for a frown instead. "Well, I'll admit that Renfield's was a long shot. If your Amazon's as feisty as she seems from your description, perhaps private salons aren't her *thing*."

"Neither are they mine, but I had the courtesy to show up on the off chance I might find her." Anthony scowled and slouched further into his chair. After he kissed a woman, he always had the courtesy to seek her out to see if she'd favor a repeat performance. Apparently his Amazon had no such courtesy.

Darling fixed him with a confused look, then threw his head back and roared with laughter. "By God, Stirling! This little minx has you panting at her heels." He sighed and brushed imaginary tears of laughter from his cheeks. "Do please wipe that dejected look off your face. You are precariously close to damaging your reputation over one elusive female. Have some pride!"

Anthony was in no mood for his friend's teasing. "I'd love some. Help me find this woman so that I can wrest mine back from her."

Darling shook his head in mock pity and clicked his tongue. "Oh pish, Stirling. We've been through some interesting times over the years, and I hope I have not misjudged you so badly as to assume that you can hold your own with a mere hoyden. You've never let a woman get the upper hand with you before. She must have caught you on an off-night, dear boy. I would hate to have to end our friendship just because you've begun to bow at the altar of woman. I simply couldn't be seen in polite company with a married man as my friend."

Anthony shrugged. Marriage was the last thing on his mind. Delicious revenge was still the first. "Don't write me off yet, Darling. I'm far too young to be thinking about the banns. Now, are you going to continue mocking me, or do you have anything helpful to say?"

Darling furrowed his brows, searching for something useful. Anthony knew he wouldn't disappoint. Darling knew everything about everyone and was an infallible judge of character. Unfortunately, or perhaps in Darling's mind, fortunately, these talents were mostly put to use seducing Bath's prettiest maidens. No woman could out-maneuver Darling's pernicious mind. Finally, his friend spoke: "Well it may be nothing again, but why don't you try the theatre tonight? It's *the* place to see and be seen, and if she's there, you'll have more than an easy time identifying her. And –" he waggled his eyebrows, "making your intentions known."

"Wonderful." Anthony loved the theatre even less than a salon. Ever since he'd bedded a potentially insane actress who had attempted to do some rather unsavory things to his male anatomy with a pair of scissors the morning after their encounter because he'd declined to become her protector, his enjoyment of the stage had been reduced to trepidation. "She had better be there. I'm becoming rather annoyed by her dashed gall in avoiding me." He stood and stalked out, but turned back at the door. "And Darling," he said, icily polite, "if you've steered me wrong again, I might just have to claim my winnings from last week's faro game. I believe you promised me a month of your Spanish mistress, fully paid?" His friend blanched at the thought of the un-recouped expense. "You had better hope I find my Amazon, or I might just be in the mood for your Jacinta."

CHAPTER FIVE

Anthony stood on the theater steps, regretting his decision to come. Theatre. Usually boring. Always predictable. Frighteningly unpredictable in bed. He shook off the memory of his "touched" actress and made his way up to his box.

He hadn't been in attendance in over a year, and his box was slightly dusty. Evidently the theatre owner didn't consider the son of an Earl important enough for the box to be spotless. He should cancel his box entirely. It was a waste of his money and his time. But perhaps tonight it would finally pay off.

He sat and surveyed the audience. The young Dowager Countess of Arlington and her son-in-law were seated in the box to the right of him and he made a polite nod in their direction, hiding a snigger. Everyone knew the Earl was bedding his younger step-mama. It was the talk of the disreputable half of the ton, though to give the Earl and his widowed mother-in-law credit, they had managed to keep gossip out of the papers. Anthony wondered how much money that had cost. Not that he would ever need to know. He enjoyed reading about his exploits in the gossip rags. Notoriety and infamy had a certain sweet appeal that privacy could not match.

He almost laughed out loud when he saw Darling and his scandalous Spanish mistress in another box. His friend was giving the courtesan's shoulder a lingering kiss as he helped her to her seat. Apparently Darling was making the most of what was perhaps his last night with his lovely Jacinta. Now *there* was a man who courted scandal and the gossip rags with even more ferocity than Anthony himself. Darling fairly fed off the unending stories of his debauches.

Anthony was so caught up in his amusement over his friend that his eyes nearly scanned over the beautiful woman taking her seat alone in the box directly across from him. It was her dress that caught his eye first. This one comple-mented her tall, statuesque figure even more than the deep purple one she'd worn two nights ago. Her body was swathed in billowing crimson silk, the V shaped neckline of her bodice creating a striking frame for her décolletage. This was a dress designed to incite the male imagination, he noted with appreciation. His Amazon was certainly well aware of her charms.

She was an enchanting vision, sitting so still and placid in the glow of the theatre's lamps. Her red hair was twisted on top of her head. A single proud red feather crowned the chignon. He was reminded of a Da Vinci painting, the Spartan and simple lines of her adornment allowing the shadows and light of her surroundings to paint her in chiaroscuro like one of the demure maidens in the Italian masters' paintings. The elegance suited her well. Mysterious and classical.

She drew a painted silk fan from her reticule as she looked around at the gathering audience. Her air was relaxed, but he recognized the look on her face: one of urgency masked by unconcern. It was the same look he'd doubtless worn a moment ago when he was looking for her. She, however, wore it with a much more anxious undertone. While his searching had been motivated by lust, hers was motivated by something more sinister. He tried to place the look in her eyes. Fear? No, too confident. Hope? Not happy enough. Anger? Impatience? Disgust? Perhaps.

The play began. Anthony's eyes remained on his target, scrutinizing her every motion. She watched the play with distracted disinterest for a while, then took to observing the audience again. She folded and unfolded her fan. She absent-mindedly picked at the feather in her hair. She frowned slightly, glanced back at the play, then back at the audience. Something in a box below Anthony's caught her eye. For a moment she stared across the theatre, then slowly shook her head as if to say *no*. She snapped her fan shut and shoved it into her reticule. She clenched and unclenched her hands, flexing her fingers against the sides of her chair.

On stage, a character screamed, drawing Anthony's attention for a moment. When he looked back to the woman's box, she was gone. He hesitated a moment, then exited his own box and headed for the foyer. She was nowhere to be seen. He hailed an usher.

"You, boy, did a woman in crimson pass through here?"

"No, Sir," the lad answered.

"Come." Anthony led the usher up to his box and pointed across to the box where the woman had been sitting. "Whose box is that?" he demanded.

"It's an open box, Sir. A Lady rented it for the evening."

"What was her name?"

"She didn't give one, Sir."

"Damn," Anthony growled. "Not even a family name?"

"No, Sir."

"Damn," he said again, grabbing his cloak and hat. "Fetch my carriage, boy. I'm leaving."

She invaded his dreams again, still and cold as stone, lying immobile in the center of his bed. He ran his fingers tentatively between her pert breasts, kissed their colorless tips. Her skin was hard and dusty under his hands. A faint heartbeat fluttered under her marble surface. He reached between her legs, seeking her warmth, and she rolled away from him. Anthony reached out to catch her...

...and fell off the bed.

"Damn," he swore.

Chapter Six

A nthony arrived at the Harrington ball the next evening as early as he dared without being presumptuous or inciting gossip. He wanted to anticipate his biting vixen's entrance, to be lying in wait by the time she was announced. However, halfway through the first set of dances, he was beginning to become impatient. He had remained in the entrance hall, chatting with friends and acquaintances as they arrived, keeping one eye on his social obligations and the other on the door. Meaning that he had been paying poor attention to both. She had not arrived yet. And it was well past the time at which fashionably late people arrived.

As the first contredanse neared its finish, his waiting came to an end. "Lady Cecilia Warenne," the steward announced, and Anthony looked up from his conversation with Admiral and Mrs. White to see her standing in the door-way, removing her cloak. She wore a simple gown of off-white silk, her gloves and shoes a matching shade. Her hair was in the severe high chignon of a few nights before, but now she had woven a wreath of small white flowers and pearls around her temple, and a few curls of fiery hair rested languidly on her forehead, lending her the air of Grecian grace she had possessed on the library balcony at their first encounter. *And in my dreams*, he thought, the memory of her touch making his chest tighten with desire. Again, no jewelry adorned her chest or stole attention from the soft curves of her breasts.

Perfect, he thought. She looked painfully angelic as she scanned the room, a demure smile playing at her lips. By the end of the night, he would steal that gentle innocence off her face. He would have her flushed and begging for him.

"Lady Cecilia Warenne…" he interrupted the Admiral's war story. "Now, why do I know that name?"

"Why that's the daughter of the late Duke of Queensbury, elder sister of George Warenne, the current Duke, who I believe is serving in the 9th Regiment against Bonaparte, isn't he dear?" the Admiral's wife chimed in. "I hear she only arrived in town a few days ago. Caused quite a stir. She hasn't been seen outside of her ancestral home since her father died. Poor thing must be quite delicate for a blow like that to keep her cooped up in the country for three years."

"She doesn't look delicate," the Admiral snorted, surveying the confident, white-clad figure. "Doesn't even have a chaperone. Disgraceful. Harrington should have her thrown out."

"Well, she does come from a family of headstrong women," Mrs. White continued. "You remember her first season, dear? Flirting with every man who came her way. It's a wonder her parents managed to get her safely back to the country before she made an utter fool of herself. And I'm still not convinced she didn't."

"Didn't what?" Anthony asked, his eyes still on Lady Cecilia.

"Well, make a, a... you know... of herself. She has been away in the country for a full *three years*," Mrs. White whispered.

"Hmmm," Anthony frowned. "If you'll excuse me, Admiral, Mrs. White. I feel it my duty to welcome Lady Cecilia back to Bath."

He strode brusquely through the throng of attendees at the entrance and caught Lady Cecilia's hand in his. "Lady Cecilia Warenne, a pleasure to make your acquaintance." He bowed low over her hand, brushing his lips against her gloved knuckles. Her eyebrows arched in surprise, and he noted that her eyes, as black as witches' candles in the darkness the night he met her, were a deep amber color that matched her hair. "Allow me to introduce myself," he continued. "Anthony Maltravers, Viscount Stirling, at your service."

After a moment's hesitation, she smiled and nodded her head in acknowledgement. "'Tis a pleasure to put a name to a face, Anthony." It was his turn to raise his eyebrows in surprise at her use of his given name. Such unseemly familiarity in such a well-bred lady. He wouldn't let her have the upper hand in their repartee, though.

"Lady Cecilia, if you are not already engaged, may I claim the next dance on your card?" he asked, tucking her arm through his and leading her through to the dance floor.

She threw her head back in a small, bubbling laugh and admonished him. "You have ambushed me at my entrance, my lord, so you know full well that I have no dances on my card as of yet. And," she added, fixing him with a look somewhat like amusement and yet disconcertingly more calculating, "I don't stand on ceremony. Especially not with men I have kissed. You may call me Cecilia."

Anthony bit back a smirk. "Well Cecilia, I claim this Gavotte, then." He attempted to lead her into the throng of couples lining up for the next dance, but she stood firm at the edge of the ballroom, her face suddenly serious.

"I'm afraid I must disappoint you," she insisted. "It is not my intent to dance at all tonight."

Anthony would not take no for an answer. In fact, he would take nothing but *"Yes, more. Please more! Oh God! Anthony!"* from this woman as an answer to anything. He pulled her gently into the dance, knowing she wouldn't risk a scene by physically refusing him. "Oh, but I insist," he whispered into her ear as he nudged her towards their starting places. She seemed to falter for a moment, her legs almost giving out under her as he pushed her into place rather more forcibly than he needed to, and when the music started, she gave the barest hint of a curtsey, bending her knees no more than a few inches, capturing his eyes in a bristling stare all the while. He was almost grateful when they began the dance and she was forced to look away from him for a moment, though dancing was far from his favorite activity in which to engage with a beautiful woman.

Cecilia moved stiffly in the steps of the dance, though it was clear she knew the steps by heart. He attempted a seductively disarming smile in her direction, but couldn't shake the stare of disdain from her face. As they came together for a promenade down the line, he leaned into her and asked, "Is something the matter, my lady? I did not think you would be offended by my presumptuousness after what happened between us two nights ago."

She pursed her lips in momentary contemplation, then looked up at him with an elegantly false smile. "Not at all," she assured him. "I do love a good Gavotte." He thought he heard a twinge of pain in her voice as they turned and promenaded back down the line. "However, my lord," she reiterated, the crisp formality with which she now addressed him causing an odd twinge of disappointment somewhere in the realm of what might be assumed to be his heart, "I am not here to dance tonight. I would appreciate it if you would release me at the end of this dance."

He cocked his head to one side and grinned. It was intoxicating to see his power over her, to see her shy away from him like a feral horse. *This* was the chase the maidens and matrons of Bath had been so unfortunately unable to provide him lately. But he wanted much more than to make her uncomfortable. He wanted to make her wantonly comfortable with him. "We shall see, Cecilia. We shall see."

They continued the dance in silence and the false smile remained on her lips though her eyes held an expression he could not decipher. When the music ended, she gave him a quick curtsey and attempted to push past him into the crowd thronging the dance floor, but he caught her waist and pulled her into him as the waltz began.

"Just one more, Lady Cecilia," he whispered, his lips brushing against the curls at her forehead as he held her closer than propriety allowed. *Let the gossips talk tomorrow*, he thought. *I will have this woman under my thumb by the morning, and then it will be left to her to make the best of a too-amorous show in the ballroom.* He expected she might fight his hold again, make the small scene of pushing him away that would cause as much speculation about their relationship as would a close waltz. But she did not push him away. Instead he felt her sag slightly into his arms, allowing him to pull her closer. Her hand on his was heavy and limp, and her legs moved clumsily as they danced. He looked down at her, but she kept her chin tucked down like the night he'd first seen her, her face almost pressed into the shoulder of his coat. He could not have expected a better result. Only two dances and already she was surrendering to his touch. He allowed his hand to slip lower on her back. Her hot breath singed him through his suddenly too tight collar, and he realized as he clung to his last ounce of self-restraint that he would have to sweep her out into his carriage sooner than he'd anticipated or he would make love to her on the dance floor. Her breasts brushed against his waistcoat as she took a deep breath and he closed his eyes for a moment, savoring the sensation as he realized that he was already doing just that. Making love to her on the dance floor. The idea was absurd and coarsely charming and he allowed himself a small chuckle. She whimpered slightly in response, muffling the sound by pressing her mouth into his collarbone.

Was she under his spell so soon? He released her waist and tipped her chin up to look into her eyes, and the stricken look of pain he found there made him freeze. There were tears at the corners of her eyes. A tremble on her lip. She took advantage of his shock to turn from him, walking swiftly through the crowd of dancers towards the edge of the room.

He watched her retreat, and frowned. A limp. He distinctly saw her limp as she disappeared amongst the attendees, and he had not once tread on her foot during their dances. Something was clearly not right with Cecilia Warenne. He should leave her to her privacy. Then again, it was his duty as a gentleman to assure himself that she was alright. She was, after all, without an escort tonight. And he had promised his pride that he would have her tonight, whether she wanted him or not. Resolute to complete his mission, he followed her out of the dance.

In his confusion he had lost her in the crowd, despite the

fact that she was as tall as half the men in attendance and taller than most of the ladies. He searched for her pearl and blossom encrusted head in the mob of young men and women all around the edge of the ballroom. A group of couples walked away from the wall onto the dance floor and he caught a glimpse of her white dress fluttering through a doorway across the room. He pushed his way through the merrymaking crowd to the place where he'd seen her disappear.

She was nowhere in sight. He slipped into the hallway, walking as quietly as he could, listening for any sound of her. Her footsteps. Her voice. There was nothing. The music from the ballroom faded as he wandered deeper into the house. He had almost decided to scrap his plan for the evening and leave it until another day when he heard voices at the end of the hall. He followed them, and finding the door into the garden at the end of the hallway ajar, he pushed it open and slid silently out into the darkness. The voices faded for a moment, then, "Where were you at Lady Spencer's?" shouted in a male voice echoed from around the corner of the house. He crept forward until he could peer around the ivy covered wall without being seen.

There she was, her thin white dress hanging limp in the damp night air, backed against the wall of the house by an angry looking man dressed in regimental reds. Their voices were hushed beyond his hearing, but she was saying something, her eyes wide and impatient. The man answered her back with a look of mocking contempt on his face and she curled her lip at him, pushing him away.

He pushed her back, holding her shoulders against the wall, and Anthony was tempted to step out of his hiding place and rescue her from her unwelcome company, but the look in her eyes as her face shone in the moonlight made him hesitate. It was not a look of fear or pleading. Not the look of a woman in danger. Her eyes flashed with defiance. She stood straighter until the height of her gaze matched her attacker's, not bothering to attempt to escape from her captor as she stared him down. She said something too quiet to be intelligible from Anthony's distance, her lips forming every word in sharp contempt. The military man looked at her silently for a moment, then grasped her left leg, digging his thumb into the inside of her thigh. She cried out in pain, her legs buckling under her as she slipped down the wall to the ground. "You will, or I will ruin you!" the man spat down at her, before turning and storming back towards the garden doors.

Anthony crouched in the shadows as the man passed, then turned back to where Cecilia sat on the ground, her teeth gritted together and eyes squeezed shut.

This was unconscionable! Anthony was well known for his abominable treatment of the fairer sex, but never had he physically attacked a woman, *injured* a woman. He strode out into the moonlight towards her, his only thoughts at that moment to sweep her up into his arms and let her weep against his shoulder.

She heard his approach and hissed "Back for it so soon?" But when she looked up and saw Anthony, a sob of relief shook her.

Suddenly, he couldn't find any words to say. He was not accustomed to comforting people. But she spoke again before he had to.

"Please," she said, her voice steadier, "bring me my cloak and arrange for my carriage to meet me at the back of the house." He stood there, unsure, still searching for some way to comfort her, but this was all so far out of his usual realm of expertise regarding women. "Please," she repeated.

"Yes," was all he managed to say.

CHAPTER SEVEN

I f he was nothing else, Anthony Maltravers was a man of action, a man who wasted no time in any of his activities: not seductions, not card games, and not rescuing beautiful women. Within five minutes he had instructed his coachman to meet him at the back of the house and retrieved Cecilia's cloak from the cloakroom.

When he met her outside she was huddled in the same position in which he'd left her, her hands pressed against her leg where the man had assaulted her. He held her cloak, offering to put it on her, and she stood, bracing herself against the wall as she straightened her legs, her hands still clutching the off-white silk around her thighs. She turned her back to him and he wrapped the black velvet material around her shoulders, his hands lingering on her chest a bit longer than was appropriate. She shrugged him off and with shaking fingers tried to tie the cloak closed at her throat. He reached out again to help her, but she shied away from him. He frowned. What was so abhorrent in accepting help freely given? But he wouldn't risk insulting her, pushing her away now by forcing more help then she asked for. Not when they were about to be enclosed in a carriage together and he might at last get a chance to employ his full charm. Finally, she pulled her gloves off in frustration and managed to tie a lopsided bow with naked fingers. Then she pulled the hood over her face and gathered the cloak tightly around herself.

He offered her his arm. "Shall we go to the carriage?"

After a moment's hesitation, she accepted the aid. "Thank you," she said, her voice stiff and strained.

As they made their way through the garden to the back of the house, she leaned on him, and when he held her around the waist, supporting her with his other arm, she did not protest. He could feel through the cloak the tightness of her abdomen as she struggled to remain upright, and wondered at the lack of softness around her waist, a softness which he had come to expect in a woman. She was hard. Not the hardness of bone, but the hardness of muscle flexing beneath skin. It was a curious feeling against the palm of his hand, as if he were supporting one of his friends after a night of heavy drinking.

Only when they had reached the carriage did she look up from the ground. "That is not my carriage," she said, her expression unreadable, her lips pursed in stoic stubbornness as they had been when he first laid eyes on her.

"No, It is mine," he answered.

She stood looking at him, clearly attempting to gauge his intent. When she made no move towards the open door of the carriage but merely narrowed her eyes distrustfully, he stepped forward and put his hand at the small of her back, pushing her gently to it. "I cannot allow you to return home alone in your present condition. I have no sinister intent regarding your person," he assured her. She didn't respond, but inclined her head in acquiescence and climbed unaided into the carriage, whispering "Sixteen Wickham Circle" to the driver.

As she did so, he thought he saw it again, the little limp she'd had when she'd escaped from him on the dance floor. Escaped? Is that how it had been? She'd escaped from one rake only to end up in the clutches of a far more violent man?

He avoided her eyes as he climbed into the coach after her, unsure what he would see and how he would react to it. Any look other than fear or pain in her eyes, and he feared he would… What? Force her there, in the carriage? The image of her pressed against the wall, defiant, stoic, not in the least bit vulnerable until that man had touched her – *touched her where I would have touched her*, Anthony thought with a shudder of guilt. *I would have been as rough with her. It was my intention tonight to be rough with her*. And though he told himself he was, if not a *gentle*man, at least better than the oaf Cecilia was tangled with, the arousal he felt betrayed him as he pictured *himself* holding her against her will against that wall, stealing the look of bravery from her eyes with a demanding grasp of her breasts, between her thighs.

He looked at her out of the corner of his eyes. She sat almost motionless, her hands still shaking as they clutched the velvet cloak around her legs. Her eyes were wide and haunted, like those of a fox who know the hounds have it cornered. He quelled a sudden impulse to pull her into his lap, let her rest her cheek against his cheek, run his fingers softly through her hair.

Damn this woman! She had the same breathless, confusing effect on him whether she was kissing him or ignoring him entirely.

In the seat across from him, Cecilia took a deep breath and exhaled it against the carriage window. "How much did you see?" she asked, her voice level and guarded.

"Enough to suspect that I am not the greatest threat you face," He replied just as evenly. He had wished to make his tone comforting, but instead the words rang haughty and judgmental in his ears. Cecilia's lips twisted in a grimace of a smile before she looked away from him again.

They rode the rest of the way to her house in silence.

Chapter Eight

W hen they arrived at Number Sixteen Wickham Circle, Anthony jumped down from the carriage and offered her his hand. Without looking at him, she ignored his help and brushed brusquely passed him to her door, unlocking it with a small key she pulled from her bodice. He was momentarily startled that no servant answered the door, and that the entrance hall and staircase of her home were lit by only a few oil lamps. Surely she did not live alone? The stories of her family's wealth were astounding.

"Shall I summon your butler, or perhaps your maid?" he asked, following her up to the door, unwilling to leave her entirely alone. Unwilling to give up the small chance of bedding her tonight he still hoped he had.

She turned to him and placed a hand firmly on his chest. "I thank you for your aid, Lord Stirling," she said, her voice brittle, "but now I must ask that you leave me to myself."

"No," he said, pushing his way through the door.

"You would enter a lady's house uninvited?" Her eyes blazed. "Leave me be, please."

"My conscience will not allow me."

"Your conscience is not needed here," she admonished him, making her way quickly up the stairs. The limp. Again. Why was she limping?

"But I clearly am."

She turned back to face him, her eyes sparking with anger. "Leave my house! Leave me be. Before my patience runs out!" she shouted, then faltered, steadying herself on the banister. Anthony made a step towards her, but stopped when she sobbed, "No!"

He watched in confusion as her hands gripped the balustrade at the top of the stairs, knuckles stark white against the mahogany. Only a half-an-hour before, it had been his intention to follow the flustered woman all the way to her bedroom, and once there… His breath quickened as his mind wandered to their scandalous meeting three evenings prior. That night, even this night, she had seemed ripe for the picking, encouraging his advances, flirting with a sort of desperate confidence that he'd assumed could only mean one thing: she wanted him, or perhaps any man, badly. But the carriage ride to her home, her behavior now, had him puzzled far beyond the state of confusion he'd ever encountered on account of a woman. Hell, he'd *never* encountered confusion because of a woman. Lust, scorn, amusement, and pity had all found their way through his hard heart during his career as one of Bath's most prolific rakes, but never confusion. Women were easy to predict and easy to manipulate. The kinds he took advantage of at least: the willing virgins and the bored society wives. He had assumed she was of the former type, but her current haste to get rid of him, and her almost venomous annoyance at his insistence to stay by her side belied more than the mere moral objections of a virgin. That, added to the look he'd seen in her eyes as she was speaking to that man not half-an-hour before, a look of fierce, lip curling hatred, her strange physical reaction when the man had grasped her thigh, and then her obvious distraction in the coach, had him paralyzed with indecision. What *was* this creature that stood before him, resembling an ill-fated Cassandra watching Troy burn, who three nights before had been a warm, passionate Cressida, her body responding uninhibitedly to his lips and hands? Dear gods, now she had him recalling Shakespeare, though he'd spent the better years of his adult life attempting to wash away his gentlemanly education in the various grimy bathtubs of whorehouses.

Above him on the stairs she shook, eyes tightening in pain. With the movement, the cloak she had kept tightly wrapped around her since their departure from the Harrington ball spilled from her shoulders.

A strangled gasp died in his throat. Blood pooled through her dress from the point on her left thigh where the man had pressed his thumb into her flesh. As Anthony watched in horror, the red stain spread further down her white skirts, soaking the hem of her dress and dripping onto the carpet. He tore his gaze from the livid stain to her face, now deathly pale, as she stared blankly at the blood seeping down her dress. Then she looked at him, her eyes empty and unemotional, and murmured, "Oh, damn." She swayed, eyelids becoming heavy, and as her fingers weakly released the balustrade, she toppled down the stairs towards him.

He remained paralyzed for another moment as she began to faint, his mind unable to wrap itself around what he had just seen. But as she fell, his body leapt into action, racing up the steps three at a time to catch her before her head hit the stairs. She slumped into his arms, her form heavier than he'd anticipated. He lifted her and was surprised again to feel the hardness of muscle in her back and legs, rather than the soft flesh he was so accustomed to on a woman. Her head nodded limply against his shoulder and she opened her mouth, a soft whimper escaping. He leaned close to catch her words. "No... doctor." she whispered.

He carried her up the remaining steps and towards the room she had been heading to, which he assumed was her bedchamber. He struggled with the doorknob, unwilling to put her down to turn it, then finally kicked the door open and laid her swiftly on the bed. She remained motionless. He pressed his fingers to the side of her neck. Her pulse was shallow and fast, but she was alive. He moved to her side, kneeling beside the bed, hands hovering over her bloody skirts. *Call a maid*, he told himself. *Call a doctor*. But before he could do the sensible thing, he was pulling up her dress to find the source of the bleeding. Her stockings and garters were red and soaked through as well, though he noted with an inappropriate tightening in his breeches that the satin garters had already been red, a delicately erotic contrast against her milky skin. He took a deep breath to calm himself. Though his reputation might be shocking, no one could accuse him of ever having ravished an unconscious woman, let alone one bleeding so profusely. Cautiously, he pushed the dress higher up on her thigh, and noted with another self-conscious jolt of lust that she was not wearing any bloomers. Her upper thigh, however, was wrapped in a coarse bandage now drenched with blood. His curiosity rather than his lust was now peaked. He lifted her knee gently and unwrapped the bandage from her leg. Underneath, her skin was slick with blood. He looked around the room for something to aid her, then grasped the basin of water and washcloth beside the bed and began to clean her leg.

As the blood was wiped away, he found the source of the bleeding. Just on the inside of her thigh was a small, ragged hole, the skin around it red and blotchy. He wiped the cloth over the wound and looked closer. He had seen just the same sort of wound two years before, when one of his friends had been fatally shot during a duel. The bullet had made the same sort of small livid hole in his friend's chest. He rocked back onto his heels and squeezed his eyes shut in confusion. What, in the name of everything sacred, was the daughter of a Duke doing with a bullet wound in her leg, and who had shot her?

CHAPTER NINE

By the time Cecilia stirred from her faint a half-hour later, Anthony had propped her torso up on the pillows at the headrest of the bed and finished cleaning her leg as best he could. The pale yellow bed covers were now stained a light orange from the bloody water, and her left stocking and shoe, along with the bloody bandage, lay crumpled on the floor. Slowly, she opened her eyes. She seemed confused as to where she was for a moment, then she looked down, saw her naked leg un-bandaged on the bed, and sat up abruptly, wincing in pain as the movement caused a fresh trickle of blood to escape from the wound. Anthony leapt up from the chair where he had been watching her and pressed her back into the pillows. She fought back for a moment, pushing him away with surprising strength, but the concerned look in his eyes seemed to pacify her and she relaxed into the cushions. She glared at him imperiously, wary and aloof, demanding he

41

speak first, as he eased back down into the chair beside her. He cleared his throat.

"Well," he managed.

She stared him down. He couldn't tell what she wanted. For him to leave? To explain? To demand explanations? He spoke again. "I swear I have not taken advantage. You need have no fear for your honor. I merely... I wished to know what was causing you pain."

She waived her hand in dismissal of his explanation as her eyes surveyed the bloodied bandage on the floor, the basin of red water and now-stained washcloth, the drops of her blood on his sleeves, then looked back up to catch his eyes again. She raised an eyebrow. "Honor," she muttered dismissively. Evidently the news that her honor was still intact was *not* what she had wanted to hear. Perplexing. He remembered her last words as she'd fainted. Ah, she must want assurance that her wound had been kept a secret.

"I did not call for a doctor, though I think it should go without saying that you should call one immediately. I was also not sure if I should call for your maid, so I didn't." He stood. "If you wish, I shall call her now."

She held up her hand to stop him. "No. Don't call for anyone. Sit down." She closed her eyes and took a deep breath.

His eyes traced her form, the ample bosom, rumpled dress and exposed leg giving her the appearance of an Oriental odalisque. He sat and crossed his legs to prevent another inappropriately timed arousal. He forced himself to focus on her face. No, that wasn't working. The unruly red curls around her forehead were just as alluring as the heaving of her chest as she breathed. He looked down at the wound in her leg and the seriousness of the situation rescued him from the appreciation of her form. "You owe me no explanation, of course," he said cautiously, "but I should dearly like to have one."

She opened her eyes, piercing him with the same unapologetic gaze he had come to expect in their brief acquaintance. "What makes you think I care a fig for my honor? That I am honorable?" she asked, avoiding his request for an explanation.

Anthony opened his mouth to answer, then sat back in surprise and closed it again. She continued. "Did the kiss I gave you at Lady Spencer's not adequately destroy what assumption of my honor you might have had? Or, if not that, the fact that I have been wandering about town without a chaperone?" She raised her eyebrow as if to challenge him to make further assumptions about her person.

After a few moments, he regained enough composure to answer, "You are the unmarried daughter of a Duke. I merely assumed."

She laughed. It was a dark hollow laugh that made him shift uncomfortably in his seat, not the feminine giggle she had made at the ball. "If half of what I've heard of your reputation is true, my lord, then you assume a very great deal." Now it was his turn to raise an eyebrow. "And yes," she said, "I am aware that in insulting your devilish reputation, I have implied my own fall from grace." There was something of a devious sparkle in her eyes now, the same knowing look that had so intoxicated him when she kissed him at their first meeting, as if she relished the sensations she conjured in his flesh. But just as he leaned forward to kiss her again, the look disappeared. She squeezed his hand where it lay on the edge of the bed. "Thank you for keeping this between us."

Anthony frowned. "I should still like to know what *this* is."

She withdrew her hand. "You were right when you said I did not owe you an explanation."

"Perhaps you do not, but as I took the time out of my evening to ensure you did not die in your own foyer, then I at least deserve the name of whoever did this to you. I assume this is related to the gentleman who evinced such an... unseemly knowledge of your person at the ball?"

She looked back to him, surprised, one hand picking at the neckline of her gown. "I didn't realize you were privy to so much of that exchange. And what would you do with such knowledge should I give it to you? Challenge him to a duel over a disagreement you know nothing about?"

"Any so-called disagreement that involves a lady being shot is no small matter."

"No," she answered hesitantly. Cecilia edged back into the pillows as if to shield herself from him. Then she looked up at him again, with that demanding, piercing gaze that never failed to imprison him. "This is a long story," she said, "and an unhappy one, and my own burden would lighten with the sharing of it. And I think, perhaps with your reputation, it would shock you much less than it would the rest of the *ton*. But if I satisfy your curiosity, I must have your word, not as a gentleman, because you hardly are one, but as the honest man who cared for me this night when I was vulnerable, that my story will be safe with you."

Anthony was intrigued. He loved good gossip as much as he loved a good woman, and this story promised to be as intriguing as the woman who told it. Even if he was honor bound to never let it pass his lips. "You have my word," he said.

She began, closing her eyes, "Then let us start from the fundamentals. I am nearly the last of my family. As I'm sure the gossip has informed you, my father died only a few years ago, and my mother has not left our country house since we buried him. She refuses to stray far from his grave. It is not my father's passing but the reason for his death that is the beginning of my story, so I suppose I must preface my tale by explaining that I was raised with more freedom and education than the average daughter of a duke. My childhood was spent in my family's country estate with my little brother, George, as my only playmate, and by the time I had my first season, I had become accustomed to having my own way in everything. Being informed by my father that I was expected to attract a wealthy match of my own nobility or above was not the sort of thing I pictured for my debut. At the time, I had aspirations to a love match. Though looking back, I did manage to confuse love and carnal pleasure rather badly." At this, she smiled slightly with the same kind of indulgent reminiscence with which he and his friends often recounted their escapades at their gentlemen's club. She continued, "I had become enamored of a young man of noble blood but far below my class whose identity, for the purposes of this story, need not be revealed. I decided that as I might not have a chance to feel love in the arms of my future husband, I should take it where I found it, while I was free enough to pursue it. And I must be blunt in saying what follows as there is no delicate way to say it." She sighed and squared her jaw. "I arranged a tryst for myself and my admirer in a brothel where I would not risk being recognized, and where I could enjoy my deflowering without interruption from my family or any of the better parts of society." Here the wicked smile played at the corners of her mouth again as she opened her eyes and looked at him. "And I most certainly did."

When the revelation forced a lustful sigh out of him, he realized he had been holding his breath. "You lost your virginity in a whore house?" he asked, his voice coarse and throaty and betraying too much shock and titillation for his taste. He swallowed and licked his lips. She was doing it again, damn her. Those knowing eyes; the way she passed her hand across her abdomen as she looked at him, apparently appreciating the effect her story was having on him. And now, of course, she made much more sense. The innocence he had assumed of her due to her unmarried position, and the way she had responded to, nay even demanded, his physical attentions during their first kiss had been impossible to reconcile.

And, to his surprise, the knowledge that this fine lady before him was not the virginal heiress society expected her to be, that he had hoped a day ago she might be, did not disappoint him. He rather relished the idea that there was at least one young woman in all of England who was not so cowed by propriety that she wouldn't take the matter of her physical pleasure into her own hands, rather than letting one of society's resident rakes snatch it from her.

Desire tightened around his chest. He wished *he* had been the one she met in that brothel. The first man to enjoy the thrill of slipping her dress off her shoulders to reveal what no man had seen before, running his fingers lightly over the soft place at the base of her throat, brushing his lips against the nape of her neck. If only he had been in town those years ago during her first season, rather than cavorting on the continent with the rather expensive mistress he'd had at the time.

She chuckled. "Is there a more fitting place?"

"A whore house?" he repeated, incredulous.

"It was deliciously forbidden: everything I wanted it to be." She fixed him with a patronizing gaze. "As someone who has made their reputation sampling all the illicit delights life has to offer, I'd expect you to understand that when one is denied something, it takes on an almost irresistible magnetism." When he only shook his head in disbelief, she continued.

"Unfortunately, my family tracked me down. They were too late, of course, but it took them most of the night to find me, and it was a rather unsavory part of town. They swept me back to the country immediately, hushed everything up very nicely…" her voice trailed off and she frowned, guilt gathering in the tears at the corners of her eyes. "By the time I recovered, my father and brother were ill. They'd caught consumption searching for me that night." She drew a shuddering breath. "Father died. George lingered on for another month or so…" She did not bother to brush away the tears that ran slowly down her cheeks into the pillows.

Then the import of what she had said struck him. George Warenne, *dead*? "I do not understand," he managed to say. "George Warenne, Duke of Queensbury, is alive. He currently serves in His Majesty's 9th Regiment."

"Ah, yes," she said, his words having a rousing effect on her as she propped herself up on her elbow amongst the cushions. Though her tears had not yet dried, she smiled the mischievous smile again, and wiped her eyes with the back of her hand. "Here is where my and George's story truly begins.

"Upon my father's death, my mother, who is as strong-willed a woman as I, became worried for our welfare. She must have known that George would not survive long, and with the sole heir gone, the ducal estates and properties would be passed to a distant cousin and she and I would be left at his mercy. She wished neither that, nor that I would have to give up the freedoms and privileges to which I had become accustomed. When George passed, she had him buried quietly on the property, and made no announcement of his death. I don't know what she intended to do beyond pretending his existence as long as she could manage, but it gave me the best, and worst, idea of my life." Her eyes sparkled.

"Which was?" he prompted, riveted.

"My brother had bought a Lieutenant's commission, much to Father's chagrin, of course, but George was always as wild as me. I—well I didn't want to go on living at the manor with all that sadness and I was angry and—I decided to take it."

"You what?" Anthony gasped.

"Relinquished my dresses, bound my breasts, and took my brother's place. It had always been George's dream to serve his country. I wanted to make his dream come true." She said it so matter-of-factly, as if she had done nothing more than alter the wallpaper in her room.

Anthony couldn't think, he couldn't breathe, he couldn't believe her. No, not her words, but *her*. She was incomprehensible. She was a woman. A wanton woman, yes, but a woman. Yet she was unlike any woman he'd ever met. She was unlike any man, too. People simply didn't do these things. Not the people he knew. "Impossible," he said.

"Hardly," she answered. "My brother and I always looked alike. As he was a year younger than I, it was easy to explain away my hairless chin and less-muscled frame as his undeveloped youth."

She paused, seemingly waiting for him to question the plausibility of her story again, but he merely shook his head and said, "Go on."

"The next year was exhilarating. Being a man was exhilarating! Training, drinking, whoring, gambling. The life of a young soldier is a charmed life indeed. I'm sure there are plenty of men who don't think that, but for someone who always wanted freedom but never truly had it, it was a beautiful life. Hard work, of course, but still free! And as I

managed to secure a private room for myself, hiding my identity was not –"

He interrupted her. "Pardon me, but whoring?"

"I played the game to the hilt," she said, her serious
expression poorly masking amusement. "In fact, I had quite a
reputation around the barracks."

Whoring? Drinking? Gambling? He had already felt her
lean muscular physique, so it was no small stretch of the
imagination to think she had been dedicated to her military
training, and he knew quite a few women with more than a
passing fondness for the bottle or the cards, but… whoring? It
was not logically possible. He squinted his eyes and rubbed
his temples. The evening was proving to be fascinating to say
the least, but he had not been filled with so many contradic-
tory emotions and thoughts since his father had sat him down
at the awkward age of eleven after catching him peeking at
one of the maids kissing a footman, and attempted to explain
the relations between men and women. That had been uncomfortable. But this was bordering on surreal. "Lady Cecilia –"

"Just Cecilia."

"Cecilia, how do you expect me to believe you had a
reputation for whoring when you are clearly not, not at all…"
he cleared his throat, " …properly equipped?"

She chuckled again. "There is much more to whoring than
shoving a foot in a boot." She smiled as the indelicate
euphemism made him raise an eyebrow. "There's lust – " here
she allowed her eyes to trail over his body, the corners of her
mouth curving up the slightest bit when her gaze reached his
groin. Involuntarily, he licked his lips. "There's confidence –
" she lifted her chin and one eyebrow ever so slightly while
the hints of desire played at her lips, looking down her nose at
him appraisingly. Anthony had the fleeting impression of
being a prize steer in an auction. "There's the knowledge of

the female body that only another female would fully possess." She ran her fingers lightly across her abdomen as she had done before, and his loins responded with expectation. "You see," she said breathily, "I haven't taken you to bed yet, but you know I will, and you know I'll be good."

He tried to breathe, but his lungs wouldn't respond. "You will?" he whispered, disturbed at how close to a plea the words were.

"Anthony," the word was a ghost of a murmur in her throat. She leaned towards him, lips open and expectant. He leaned forward to meet her. "It is a very simple game indeed." Then the little wicked smile spread across her face and she fell back into the cushions, laughing.

"I see." He sat back in his chair, attempting to look as casual as possible. Damn the chit, she had him eating out of her hand! She knew it and she was enjoying it! He folded his hands over his lap to cover his erection. He had to distract her from his helplessness by bringing her back to her story. "Seduction is one thing, Cecilia, but how, pray tell, did you perform the acts necessary to build up a reputation?"

"You men are all so convinced your cocks are God's gift to womankind, you forget there are other avenues to pleasure," she scoffed.

"You don't mean—"

Cecilia rolled her eyes. "I was the rare sort of man prostitutes dream of. The offer of pleasure with no expectation of return... I was a favorite client."

"I don't believe you," Anthony said. It was a lie. Unbelievable as it might seem, he had no doubts about her story. It was incomprehensible. Fascinating. Utterly ludicrous. Scandalous. Cecilia. He was beginning to sense a pattern.

"You wouldn't be the first man to think his prick was solid gold," she said, deliberately misunderstanding him. She laughed. "But if more men followed my example, there would be a great deal more satisfied women. It nearly got to the point where prostitutes were soliciting *me*." She smiled and shook her head. "Good days they were. But nothing lasts forever, and happiness doubly so." She sighed and steeled herself to go on.

"We were called to battle. I knew, when I joined, that we were in the middle of a war with Napoleon. But I never thought I'd have to fight." A look of sudden realization flickered across her face. "Then again, perhaps I did. Perhaps I took that commission because I couldn't find anything left to live for and I wanted a bit of a lark before I made my grand goodbyes. That or I was so much more naïve than I would like to admit now." She looked at Anthony, her gaze hollow and hypnotizing. "Have you ever been to war, Anthony?"

He had to be honest. "No."

"I wouldn't recommend it. Not only is it the most useless, sickening, insufferable waste of human effort," she fairly spat out the words, "but life on the campaign made hiding my femininity nearly impossible. I couldn't bathe regularly. We all smelled a mess, but a woman's smell is different from a man's. I was sure every time I walked past one of the men, he'd know. I decided I'd made a mistake. That I would request a transfer back to London. I was playing the role of a duke; I didn't think it would be hard to take the coward's way out with my family name to back me up. But then, this..." she pulled her left sleeve down, revealing a long pink scar, the mark of a bullet or perhaps a sabre cut just below the shoulder. "Some of the men got much much worse. Men who had been my friends. George's friends. So I did the foolish thing and stayed. And that's when *he* found me out."

He. She said the word as if she were naming the devil. "The man I saw with you tonight?" Anthony asked.

She nodded. "Captain Brinkley. He noticed my hesitance to let the doctor see to my wounds. He came into my tent while I was trying to bandage myself, and…" The façade of confidence on Cecilia's face faltered for a moment as her lips curled back in the same disgusted sneer she'd cast at Captain Brinkley at the ball that evening. "Being a committed opportunist, he demanded a price for his silence."

Anthony had no words for this sort of situation. He knew what price she meant. The price no man should demand from a woman. Not a gentleman, and not even a rake. A rake took what was freely given, but he did not steal. He watched, helpless, as Cecilia bit back tears, her hand rubbing her chest absentmindedly as she struggled to breathe. On instinct, he reached out and grasped her fingers, holding them steady. She flinched once, then stilled, her breathing calming under his touch. Self-conscious at his rare kindness, Anthony tried to pull away, but she held his hand against her chest. The warmth seeping through her bodice burned him. The heat was exquisite.

"There is not much more to tell," she continued, her voice returning to its matter-of-fact timbre. "Our arrangement went on until a month ago, when Captain Brinkley was given leave and sent here. I knew I had to follow him to make sure he stayed silent. Not long ago, I was shot in battle and fell unconscious. When I woke, I found I'd been left for dead on the field. So I let George stay dead there, and I pawned my sabre and the buttons from my regimental jacket to make my way back to England. And the rest you have been privy too. I have spent the last four days attempting to persuade Captain Brinkley to leave George for dead, as I have done, but he is a stubborn man."

Anthony squeezed her hand in his. His attention to her story was no longer plagued by lust. He still felt it of course.

Lady Cecilia was no less beautiful then when he'd first seen her, and certainly more fascinating. But now, he discovered, he had respect for her.

Respect for a woman. The feeling was fresh and strange. He enjoyed it. And how could he now enjoy bending Cecilia to his will when he felt such a need to protect her, to keep her from the sort of treatment even he would never have inflicted? Well, that finally quashed the last of his hopes to… to do whatever it was he had intended to do with her before he knew.

"What will you do now?" Anthony found himself asking.

She gave him a searching look, pressed his hand harder against her bosom, then fixed him with a pleading smile. "I will ask you ever so politely to take the bullet out of my leg. I have tried, but I cannot focus through the pain."

He drew back. "Beg pardon?"

"The bullet is still in my thigh, Anthony," she said, slowly and clearly as if he was stupid and she was merely asking him to pass the strawberry jam. "Please take it out."

He shook his head. Cleaning up all the blood had almost been more than he could handle, and the thought of causing her further pain made his bile rise. Not to mention the fact that he had no medical training. And this whole evening must be some dark and unforgivably frustrating dream. He would wake up in the morning with a hangover and find that Lady Cecilia was just another flirtatious debutante. Oh, but that would be too simple, wouldn't it? Cecilia did not seem like a simple woman. "Call a doctor."

"No doctors. No one must know. There are tweezers on my nightstand and knives and towels aplenty in the wash-room from the last time I tried. You could have it done in five minutes."

He stood to leave. He was sure if he stayed a moment

longer in her presence he would either vow to be her knight in shining armor until the end of time or ravish her there on the bed, surrounded by bloody sheets. Neither option seemed like a remotely good choice. "Lady, Cecilia, you –"

"I've told you," she said with a gentle smile, "call me Cecilia."

"Cecilia, you ask too much of me. I cannot – it would cause you pain."

She sat up on the bed and grasped his wrist as he tried to walk away. His eyes met hers and for a moment she left the depth of her suffering and loneliness unmasked. The slight twitch of her lip as she begged him was a siren call. He could not look away. "Please, Anthony. Nothing you could do to me could hurt more than—than what has already been done to me." Her mouth twisted in a wry smile. "Please."

"I…" he began, but he could make no more refusal. He simply stared at her, at the ghost of hope he saw dancing across her amber eyes.

"Help me."

Yes. He nodded. *Always, yes.*

CHAPTER TEN

"Are you ready?" Anthony asked, his voice wavering. He had placed a clean cloth beneath her leg, and the tweezers and smallest kitchen knife were laid out on the bed. He moved the candles on the bedside table closer to give himself more light. *Idiot*, he thought. *Call a doctor, you idiot. You cannot do this without hurting her*. Then again, he didn't want anyone but himself ever touching her again.

"I have been through war, my lord. I am ready for anything." She met his uncertain gaze with confidence, and clutched one of the cushions to her chest. "Do it quickly before I lose my nerve and allow you to call a doctor."

He stared down at her leg, at the pale skin, the red wound, the impatient muscles tensed in anticipation. He picked up the knife and took a deep breath, steeling his nerves. Bending his head over the wound, he used the flat of the knife to push aside the broken skin, searching for the bullet. Breath hissed between her teeth and her leg jerked slightly. He couldn't bring himself to look at her face, but asked, "Are you alright?"

"Hurry up," she answered. He could hear her grind her teeth together as he probed further. The point of the knife tapped against something hard. In the faint glow of the candles, he could just make out the dull round shine of the shot. Keeping the knife in place to hold her skin out of the way, he reached for the tweezers with his other hand and dug into the wound. A strangled whimper escaped from her throat. Christ, he was going to Hell for this. The tweezers slipped in the lesion, unable to gain purchase on the musket ball, and the blood pooling out onto the towel blocked his ability to see anything. He blindly pinched the tweezers down again and managed to catch the offending object. She cried out, the sound muffled into the pillow. Slowly, carefully, he pulled the musket ball free.

"It's done," he whispered, looking up at her. She had bit down on the pillow to stifle her cries, and her eyes were shut tightly, tears running down her cheeks. He dropped the knife and tweezers and cupped her face between his hands, willing her to look up at him, desperate to comfort her. She was trapped in her own vulnerability now, the same way she'd been when Captain Brinkley had re-opened her wound a few hours earlier. "Cecilia?" he asked. She whimpered again and looked up at him. "It's done. It's finished," he reassured her.

"I was wrong," she choked, the words half sob and half laugh. "This hurt just as much."

She smiled at him, a smile of gratitude and trust that warmed him all the way through to his selfish heart. She took his hand in her own and kissed his palm, her eyes never leaving his. "I am very, very glad you forced your way into my house tonight."

The blood from his hand glistened against her lips, dark and mesmerizing. He reached for the towel and wiped her face and his hands, lingering over her mouth. He brushed her lips again with his fingertips. So soft. How could anyone have ever thought she was a man? No man could have lips so soft.

She reached up and pulled his face down to hers, giving him no time to protest, stealing his willpower with her heat and softness before he could pull away. He kissed her gently, reverently, worshipping her mouth. Her tongue darted out and sought the place on his lower lip where she had bit him three nights before, exploring the dainty tooth marks.

Before he could break the kiss and insist that she rest, she sank back into the cushions, pulling him on top of her. She laced her fingers through his hair and held his mouth to hers. His body acted on instinct, crawling onto the bed and straddling her, keeping his lips locked with hers, his tongue exploring the soft feminine taste of her. She moaned low in her throat and his member began to swell at the sultry sound. He reached one hand up to her breasts, fingering her pert nipples through the silk of her gown. No stays, only a chemise, he realized with a quickening pulse as he massaged her through the thin fabric.

The thin *bloody* fabric. She purred, her lips forming into a smile against his and he groaned, pushing himself off her.

"We must stop," he gasped. His cock throbbed in his breeches. The need she incited in him was anguish, but he would not make love to her like this. He wouldn't risk causing her pain again. She sighed and nodded and reached out for his hand, lacing her fingers through his.

"But will you stay with me tonight?" she asked, her voice rough with want.

He squeezed her hand and lay back on the bed next to her.

"Not even the Devil himself could tempt me away." He meant it. There was nothing he wanted more than to be next to her. Except to be inside of her. His whole body wanted that, wanted it to the point where his bones ached and his hands shook. But if he couldn't have that, he would settle for the next best thing. She smiled and closed her eyes. He took a deep breath, absorbing her scent: blood and sandalwood soap and graceful femininity and anguish and courage. *Cecilia.*

He closed his eyes and drifted off to sleep, still holding her hand.

CHAPTER ELEVEN

M orning light was pouring through the open curtains of Cecilia's bedroom. Anthony stirred and stretched. The hand that had held hers last night was now empty. Eyes still closed against the invading sun, he reached out for her. The bed beside him was empty too.

Anthony sat up. The coverlet, stiff with dried blood, lay crumpled at the foot of the bed. Cecilia's ruined silk gown from the night before was flung over the back of a chair. She was nowhere to be seen. He smoothed back his rumpled hair and loosened his cravat. Something crunched under his hand. He looked down to find a small piece of paper pinned to his collar. *Kitchen*, it read.

Anthony had never been into the kitchen of even his own house. He wandered through Cecilia's townhouse, starting with the upper floor, then making his way down to the first. Each room he inspected was empty and silent. White sheets shrouded all the chairs and tables. Dust covered everything. There were no servants anywhere. It looked as if the house had lain empty for years. Well, ever since Cecilia had decided to become a Duke and take up arms. He chuckled into the silence. Last night hadn't satisfied his body as he'd hoped it would, but it had certainly been interesting.

On the ground floor, he could hear the noise of pots and pans. He made his way down the servants' back hallways until he found the source of the noise. Cecilia was standing in the kitchen, clothed in a nightgown and a man's greatcoat, her red hair falling loose about her shoulders. Her hair was no longer than her shoulder blades. She must have cut it when she first took her brother's commission. She was slicing pieces of bread from a hard brown loaf. He stood in the doorway and watched her. She limped to the stove and checked the coffee pot to see if the water was boiling, then eased herself into a chair, favoring her left leg as she sat and chewed on a crust of bread.

"Good morning," Anthony said, moving to sit beside her at the kitchen table.

"Good morning!" She smiled up at him in surprise. "I was beginning to think you'd sleep through the whole day."

"What time is it?"

"Almost noon."

"Why didn't you wake me?"

She cocked her head to one side, bemused. "I thought I should let you sleep. I did rather abuse what little good nature you possess last night."

He frowned at her. "You are the one who fainted from loss of blood, and you were worried about *me* losing sleep?"

She laughed and stood to pour the coffee, but he pushed her back down into her chair. "I'll do that. You rest."

"I am not dying, you know," she said, annoyed, then

caught his hand in hers and nestled it against her cheek. "Thanks to you, my lord."

He couldn't tell if there was a hint of humor in her voice, or if she was sincere. "Considering our tumultuous acquaintance, don't you think using polite titles is just a bit... ludicrous?"

She tossed his hand away and laughed again. "Pour me some coffee, Anthony. I'm parched."

He chuckled. He loved her directness, her lack of guile. She was an enigma, to be sure, but not a self-conscious one. She did not practice to deceive. She merely lived as she wished, society and everyone else be damned. And she had suffered for it. Anthony surprised himself by thinking it should not be so. Why should she suffer because she'd chosen to make her own destiny, as sordid and shocking as it was? She had fought for her country and that alone, her elegance, courage, and independence aside, made her worthy of the highest esteem and praise, despite what anatomy she had hidden underneath her regimental reds. Were she a man, he wouldn't hesitate to call her a hero.

Darling was right to worry about his reputation. He was taking a woman's side. Next thing he knew, he would be married, dandling a babe on his knee while Cecilia went shooting.

Inconceivable. He poured them each a cup of coffee and sat down again at her side.

"Cecilia," he asked, gently laying a hand on her knee, "why is your house empty?"

She shrugged. "I've barely been back in town a week. I do have a coachman and a maid permanently employed here, but they're rarely about. I just haven't had the time or the inclination to re-staff my household." She sipped her coffee and sighed. "I've been planning on returning to my family's country estate when... my business is finished here."

"That brings me to a more important question. What *is* your business here?"

She avoided his eyes and took a bite of bread. "Captain Brinkley is my business."

Anthony caught her chin in his hands and pulled her towards him until her lips almost brushed his. "That is not a satisfactory answer, Cecilia." He teased her with a light kiss. "Be warned that I am not above kissing the answer out of you."

She pulled away from him and shot him a scolding glance. "Be warned that it will not work. Nor is it your business. It is mine."

He couldn't resist the foolhardy urge to be her protector, though she clearly wanted none of it. "And if I wish to make it mine?"

She stood and clasped his hands in hers. "You have done so much for me in only the last ten hours. I will not ask more of you." She turned from him and made her way slowly and painfully to the kitchen door. He rushed after her and swept her into his arms.

"Where are you going?"

She raised an eyebrow in amusement. "I should like to rest." Placing a hand firmly on his chest, she said, "Alone."

He smiled ruefully. She was right, of course. "Very well, my lady," he acquiesced. "Will you at least allow me to carry you to your room?"

She planted a soft, lingering kiss on his neck. "It would be as much my pleasure as yours, my lord."

CHAPTER TWELVE

An hour later, Anthony joined his friend for an excessively late breakfast at their club. Darling raised his eyes from his plate and shook his fork reprovingly at Anthony.

"No, no, no. It was a fair bet, but I'm not giving up Jacinta. You'll have to find someone else."

Anthony laughed. "Relax, Darling. I've no intention of taking you up on your offer of your mistress. It just so happens that I found my Amazon."

His friend's face relaxed into a mischievous smile. "Do tell."

Anthony opened his mouth for a moment, then closed it again. He had sworn that nothing Cecilia had told him would pass his lips. And even if he had not sworn, he would be damned if he told Darling anything important. The man's mouth was looser than a whore's morals. "There isn't much to tell, Darling. The lady is magnificent. I shall leave it at that."

"Do I detect a hint of infatuation, there, old chap?" Darling asked, taking a bite of his ham.

"I don't know, Darling, and I don't care. As I said, the lady is magnificent."

"So you bedded her, then."

Before Anthony could stop himself, the words popped out: "No, I didn't."

Darling's fork and knife fell to the table with a clatter. "Why ever not, you great dunderhead?"

Anthony shrugged. He owed his friend no explanation. And he didn't have one that didn't involve explaining that the woman he'd intended to bed was a wounded soldier.

"You are giving the time-honored title of rake an abysmally weak reputation, Stirling! I don't care to see what comes next. Starting a charity? Taking a vow of abstinence? *Marriage*, for God's sake?" Darling shook his head in disgust and took another bite of ham. "The only way I can possibly excuse you is if the lady in question isn't actually a lady at all. No chance she's a man, I suppose?"

Anthony hefted his hands in front of his chest, making the universally vulgar sign for breasts, and shook his head.

"Ah, yes," Darling continued, "you did mention her bosoms before. Could still be a man, you know. The Greeks used to have a name for something of that kind, didn't they? Men with the body of a woman? *Venus Androgynous* or something of the sort. Worshipped them, if I recall."

Anthony closed his eyes and images of Cecilia's leg flooded his mind. Her naked thigh, bared up to the hip, and perhaps a bit further. Though his chivalry towards the wounded siren made it impossible to admit aloud, he had seen enough to know she was equipped with the set of parts complementary to that which resided in his trousers. "She's not a man, Darling."

"Pity. It would seem then, Stirling, that you've truly lost your touch."

"Hmm?" Anthony asked, his mind still occupied with thoughts of Cecilia's leg. And the rest of her body that was attached to it... If only he'd managed to "accidentally" see her breasts as well while she was unconscious, but, damn his newfound morality, it hadn't even occurred to him at the time.

"Never mind, you disgustingly love-sick whelp," Darling spat. "Are you going to eat something, then? Because if not, I'd rather sit alone and bemoan the loss of all my friends to matrimonial misery then share this table with you and your shrinking masculinity."

"I'm not hungry," Anthony answered with a grin. "I just breakfasted on coffee and stale bread made by the loveliest woman in Bath. I can't think of anything more celestially fill-ing." He *was* hungry, truth be told, but oh how he loved that bewildered look on his friend's face.

Darling rolled his eyes. "Get out, then. Get out. You're spoiling my mood. All this tediousness has put me off my ham."

CHAPTER THIRTEEN

Anthony was loathe to go back to Cecilia's that afternoon both out of fear that he might hurt her with his ardor, as well as puzzlement over Lord Darling's words. Love? Surely not. The strongest sensation he felt for Cecilia was still lust: burning, consuming lust. Secondary to that was the wish to protect her, prevent her from ever suffering anything more than his own attentions. Not that she would have to suffer those. She would doubtless enjoy them. But love? He didn't know what that felt like, considering the stale demonstration of matrimony his parents had given him before his mother had died of a frozen heart due to his father's mercenary coldness. But whatever love was, it had to be more than lust and protectiveness, didn't it?

For lack of anything else to do, he spent the afternoon at his gymnasium, but four hours of being pummeled and punched did nothing to lessen his need to be in Cecilia's company. She'd bared her soul to him, but there was still so much he wanted to know, see, touch. His every thought was plagued by fantasies of her. Cecilia lounging in a bathtub, tendrils of steam caressing her face and neck. Cecilia, beckoning him to her bed, clothed in nothing but stockings and red garters. Cecilia, writhing in passion beneath him as he ground his hips into her. Cecilia, crying out for release, biting down on his shoulder as he brought her to the pinnacle of sexual satisfaction. The images returned unbidden again and again as he bathed off the sweat of his exercise, as his valet dressed him, as he sat alone at dinner, wishing every mouthful could be her lightly freckled skin under his lips. He couldn't keep himself away from her a moment longer. She was sensual, she was dangerous, she was delicious. She was a completely unique being in a town full of utterly boring and predictable people. She made him feel alive when he was near her. He needed her.

When he arrived at her house, he found the front door unlocked and the house as empty as it had been the night before. "Cecilia?" he called up the darkened staircase.

A minute, two minutes of silence, passed. "Cecilia!" he called again. She did not answer.

An elderly woman in a maid's uniform poked her head out of the servants' quarters. "Can I 'elp you?" she asked.

This must be the maid Cecilia had spoken of. "I am looking for your mistress."

"She's not at 'ome." The old woman turned to leave.

"Where is she?" Anthony demanded.

"Ain't my business to know. Or yours I should think," the maid reproached him. "Lady Cecilia's business is her own, and she don't need no one meddlin'." With that, she turned back towards the kitchens and closed the door behind her.

So Cecilia was out. Taking care of business. Anthony knew what that meant. Cecilia was away from his sphere of protection. Taking care of Captain Brinkley. Damn that filthy snake of a man! Damn Cecilia for being so proud, for not letting him help her. He turned to leave.

The image of Cecilia lying in bed swam before his eyes again. She was crying out, not in pleasure but in pain, as Captain Brinkley pinned her down. She scratched his back and he laughed at her, his amusement dark and hollow and sadistically pleased. Tears made their way slowly down her cheeks as he thrust into her; her chest heaved against his hands, struggling for breath. Her lips formed a single, pleading word: *Anthony*.

Anthony's teeth clenched. The ache in his jaw brought him swiftly back to the present, but he could still hear her plaintive whisper in his ears. *Anthony*. He shook his head, refusing to listen. *Anthony*. No. *Help me*.

His resolved faltered. Whether she wanted his help or not, she needed him. And he needed her. Needed her to be safe, happy, free from pain. To be in his arms. He took the stairs two at a time up to her bedroom.

That's where she found him an hour later, sitting on the small chair beside her dressing table. She didn't seem surprised when she opened the door. She gave him a sad nod and turned away to remove her pelisse and bonnet. He had wanted to stand and wrap her in his arms the moment she entered, assure her that he was there to protect her and that he would never leave, but now he found himself frozen in his seat. Offering to defend her would patronize her. With her strong will and independence, he would insult her beyond reparation; she would never speak to him again. And he could not let that happen. He couldn't lose her to her own pride or his own foolishness.

"I know where you were," he said slowly, careful to keep reproach out of his tone.

She turned to him, slipping her yellow silk dress over her shoulders and down to the floor. Her lip quivered as she made a resigned sigh, but she denied nothing. Her hands were shaking, and she gripped the thin fabric of her chemise to keep them steady.

He forced himself to stay in his chair.

Through the chemise, he could make out the shadow of red curls between her legs, the bright white of a clean bandage wrapped around her thigh, the rosy pearls of her nipples showing through the cloth in the candlelight. He willed himself not to breathe, not to become aroused. She stared into his eyes, her face a veneer of statuesque indifference, and he wondered if she could sense his lust.

"I am staying with you tonight." He forced the words out one by one, digging his fingers into the arms of the chair, trying to bring his attention away from the insistent throbbing between his legs. "Do not try to chase me away, Cecilia."

She strode slowly to him, her little limp eclipsed by the languorous undulation of her chemise against her legs. She straddled him and sat on his lap, cupping his chin in her hands and forcing him to look her in the eyes. He gave a little gasp as his cock responded to the heat of her most private place against his trousers, and she responded by angling her hips into his, pressing herself further against him. Her eyes were bursting with a wild hunger, and she parted her lips slowly, her breath tickling the hairs on his forehead.

"If you are staying the night," she whispered. "Then I must inform you that I sleep in the nude." Her hands relinquished his face and unpinned his cravat, tossing it aside. Leisurely, she unbuttoned his waistcoat and jacket and pulled them off. If his arms hadn't felt like lead, he would have helped her. When he was naked to the waist, she bent and ran her lips along his collarbone, murmuring her words into his flesh. "And you will be expected to do the same."

He could take no more. He lifted her and carried her to the bed, dropping her among the cushions, then tore off his clothes. She called him to her with the seductive curve of one finger, and he knelt on the bed beside her, crushing her to his chest and kissing her. Every nerve in his body tingled at her touch as she ran her hands down his back and up his sides, finally coming to rest on his chest. She pushed him back into the pillows and straddled him again, hitching her chemise up around her waist. Arching over him, her hair falling about his face, she kissed his jaw, his neck, his chest, teasing his nipples with her tongue. He groaned and his cock hardened further, straining against her. Dear God, she was already wet. He pulled the chemise over her head—Christ, she was beautiful, his fantasies didn't compare— and ran his hands down her torso, feeling the softness of her heavy breasts (how had she ever hidden these?), tracing the grooves of the muscles in her abdomen, squeezing her firm buttocks.

"Make love to me," she moaned, her voice ragged with desperation. "Touch me. Fill me. Wash him out of me. Please. I want to be free of him."

He obeyed, lifting her hips and easing into her, driving up until the tip of his cock pushed against her womb. She sat up and arched her back, rocking her hips against him, fingers splayed for balance against his chest. He anchored his fingers in the soft flesh of her bottom, pulling her down onto him with each thrust, massaging her thighs as he savored the slick tightness of her sheath around him. Inadvertently, his fingers rubbed against the bandage on her leg, and she winced in pain.

"I'm sorry," he gasped. "I'm sorry. I wasn't thinking –"

Silencing him with a hand over his mouth, she whispered, "Shhhh…" She guided his errant hand to the damp cleft between her legs, pressing his fingers against her bud. Instinct chased away his fear of hurting her, and he circled gently with his thumb. She whimpered and swayed her hips into his hand as she rode him. "Anthony," she begged, in the same breathless tone he'd heard her use in his fantasies. It was a request, a plea, an order to finish her. He bucked his hips against her faster, the tightness of her sex and the frantic pace hastening his own climax. The beginning tremors of her orgasm tightened the muscles of her belly and she clenched around him. He gritted his teeth, willing himself to hold out another minute, the desperate heat building low in his abdomen. Their breath came in shallow gulps. She gripped his forearms, steadying herself as her body trembled and a tense moan escaped her lips. He pulled her hips down onto him for one final thrust as he spilled inside of her. *Oh G—!* His teeth ground together. His jaw ached.

It was worth the wait. She was worth the twenty-nine year wait that had been his life. Had he ever actually made love to another woman? He couldn't remember. If he had, it certainly hadn't been like this.

For a moment, she stayed straddling him, eyes closed, clutching his arms so tightly that he began to lose sensation in his hands. He held perfectly still, forgetting to breathe, as he memorized every sensation of their coupling. Then Cecilia eased herself down beside him and draped her arm over his chest, resting her injured thigh on his abdomen.

He looked down, taking his first shaky post-coital breaths, and watched as a small bloom of crimson pushed through the fabric of the bandage. "I've hurt you," he whispered.

She looked up into his eyes and smiled, her cheeks and

lips flushed with satisfaction. "Never." She shook her head. "From the moment we met, you have done nothing but help me." She rested her head on his shoulder and brushed a light kiss behind his ear. "You aren't half the devil they say you are, Anthony Maltravers."

Chapter Fourteen

Anthony woke to Cecilia's stirrings beside him. Her hand trembled sleepily over his pectoral muscles and her naked thigh brushed against his groin as she shifted position in his arms. Opening his eyes to the late morning glow peeping through the bedroom curtains, he ran his hands down her back and caressed her rump playfully, drinking in the sight of her bare body bathed in golden sunlight. She snuggled into his embrace, her full breasts pressing into his ribs. He kissed her softly on the nose and she opened her eyes, purring deep in her throat. The signature wicked smile played at the corners of her lips and she ran her hand down his chest, over his abdomen where the deep, satisfied feeling of last night's love-making still warmed him, and rested it over his member.

He chuckled. "Don't worry, he's still there, at your service whenever you wish, my lady."

She smiled and sighed and closed her eyes again. He brushed her hair away from her cheek.

"Cecilia…"

"Hmmm?"

"I have questions."

She looked up at him in surprise. "Oh?"

He laughed. "I merely wish to know more of you."

She grinned and gave his cock a little squeeze. "I should think you know all of me by now."

He pulled her hand away from his groin and held it in his. She moaned in disappointment. He tried not to let her see the lust surging through his veins. He wanted her again. And again and again. He wanted her now. But he wanted to know some things first. He started with a harmless question. First step in any seduction: put the woman at ease. "Why do you always wear silk?"

She looked up, astonished, then laughed. "When I was George, when I had to hide my womanhood, I made myself two promises. One was that I would never, ever constrict my breasts again. The second was that I would never wear anything coarser than silk once I returned to being a woman." She leaned her face up to his and kissed him, letting her lips linger for a moment. He pulled away.

"Why did you kiss me the first night we met?"

"Because I wanted to." She smiled wantonly again and wriggled against him, rubbing her nipples into his ribcage. He sucked in his breath but held himself back from responding.

"Why did you tell me your story?"

Her eyes became serious, losing their mischievous sparkle. "I, I'm not…" She paused, seeming to search for the right words. "I understood you, from that first dance, and when you brought me my cloak and took me home. I thought that if I gave you what you needed, you would help me."

He pulled away. She sounded like she was selling herself to him. "What I *needed*?"

"Yes." She licked her lips nervously.

He sat up, pushing her off him. "And what, pray tell, is it that I *need*, Lady Cecilia?"

She rolled away and stalked off the bed, throwing him a reproving glance, and pulled on her chemise.

Anthony would not give up so easily. She was using him. It was a new sensation, and not a pleasant one. "Please. Enlighten me. What do I need?"

She limped to the chair by the bed and sank down, covering her face with her hands. "Don't be this way."

"Is it sex? Is that what I need?" The indignation in his tone surprised him. It *had* been what he wanted, after all. Sex. With her. She didn't respond. "Look at me."

Her lip curled up and she turned away. "Do not presume to order me about in my own house."

He stood and yanked on his breeches. "Do not presume to know my needs."

"I knew your reputation." Her voice was almost pleading. He wouldn't let himself look at her. He was no primitive animal, obsessed with nothing but rutting. Well, perhaps he was, but it was damned insensitive of her to call him out on that.

"So you gave me sex in return for what, Cecilia? I must know," he spat.

"I didn't say sex," she spat back. "You put those words into my mouth."

"You didn't deny them." He pulled on his shirt and waistcoat.

"Perhaps I was wrong to trust you." Her voice was level and edged with distaste.

Anthony grabbed her by the shoulders, hauling her to her

feet. "What did you expect, knowing my reputation?" She shrank away from him but he pulled her into him, holding her prisoner against his chest. "I am no knight in shining armor, Cecilia!" She flinched and tried to turn away. He saw a flicker of fear in her eyes as she blinked back tears, and he released her, regret washing over him. For a moment, he'd forgotten that she'd been forced, subjected to the basest desires of man. And now she was feeling their brunt at the hands of a man she'd trusted. He opened his mouth to apologize, but she spoke first.

"Get. Out."

"Cecilia —" he reached out to brush the tears from her cheeks but she ducked under his arm and out of his reach.

"Get out now."

Her voice trembled, but whether with rage or with fear he could not tell. He couldn't bring himself to look at her. He had surely hurt her now as much as Captain Brinkley had, and he didn't want to see the betrayal in her eyes. It already seared his back, her anger digging nails of remorse into his heart. He collected the rest of his clothing and turned the doorknob. Then he paused. He still had one more question, but he dreaded the answer. He looked back at her. She met his gaze, defiant.

"What do you plan to do about Captain Brinkley?"

A mask of indifference fell over her countenance; she squared her shoulders.

"Out."

He turned and left.

CHAPTER FIFTEEN

"I threatened her, and I insulted her beyond apology. I probed into her privacy though I knew she did not wish it. And I managed to push her away, quite expertly. Now what do I do to remedy all that?" Anthony stood in front of his mirror, savagely tying his cravat, then pinning it unmercifully down. His reflection, angry and defiant, stared back at him, offering no advice.

"I beg your pardon, my lord?" His valet mumbled, the man's hands fluttering about Anthony's collar uncertainly, clearly wishing to re-tie the lumpy cravat but not daring.

Anthony huffed and massaged his temples. "I wasn't talking to you, Smithers."

"My apologies, my lord."

"If only it were that simple: apologize," Anthony sighed, pushing his hair back from his face with more force than was needed. "But I don't think she'd accept any apologies from me with any more courtesy than a musket-ball between my eyes." He laughed an empty, hopeless laugh.

"My lord?" The valet sounded concerned.

"Irony, Smithers. Cruel, fickle irony. Or perhaps not. Perhaps I am using the meaning of irony wrong. But then I never cared much for book learning." He growled and pulled on his waistcoat. "Perhaps if I had, I'd understand her a little better." His voice softened. "She's like a Greek tragedy, you know. So stoic and determined –"

The memory of her face as she'd ordered him out of her house that morning cut his sentence short. Was that what he'd seen, a flash of grim determination concealed so well underneath that imperturbable mask? It was, damn it, it was! Determination to take her destiny into her own hands, as she had told him only two nights ago she was already so used to doing. And that meant...

"Dear God, no."

"Beg your pardon, my lord?" The valet asked again.

"Change of plans, Smithers. I will not be dining at my club tonight. I shall be attending the Whitford ball instead."

"Yes, my lord. May I suggest the dark blue crushed velvet jacket?"

"By all means, and quickly. I have to get there before she does something she'll regret."

Chapter Sixteen

"Good evening, Lord and Lady Whitford. Your home looks enchanting this evening." Anthony sketched a bow, taking his hostess's hand and gallantly kissing the air above her fingers.

"What a pleasure to have you with us, Lord Stirling," Lady Whitford simpered. "We did not expect your company this evening."

"No indeed. When I sent my regrets last week I was feeling a bit ill, but I am much recovered and I thought I should make an appearance, as there is often a dearth of gentlemen to dance with the ladies at these sorts of events." *Insufferable twits*, Anthony thought. *Where is Cecilia?*

"How thoughtful of you, my lord. I'm sure the ladies will be gratified by your consideration."

Anthony bowed again. "Indeed, Lady Whitford." He

excused himself from the receiving line and pushed his way through to the ballroom.

The first set of dances had yet to begin, and the room was crowded with young men and women eager to find a partner. He had no trouble spotting her. She stood tall and aloof in the multitude, her height and regal bearing giving her the appearance of a Goddess thronged by worshippers. He tried to breathe but found he had lost the ability. She was nothing less than stunning tonight, her Grecian form dressed to perfection in a daring gown cut from a shade of shimmering peacock indigo silk that made her skin appear even more creamy white and her mane more fiery red. The simple twist of her hair was adorned with a thin gold circlet, and she cooled herself with a fan of peacock feathers that would have looked unforgivably garish on any other woman.

Young gentlemen swarmed around her, hanging on her every word as she made what appeared to be a demure joke. The gentlemen laughed politely and Cecilia hid her insincere smile behind her fan. She looked every inch the delicate, polite maiden. Anthony knew better. Though she listened to the young bucks around her, she was looking for someone. And he knew who.

Anthony approached just as one of the young men was begging the privilege of the first dance. Cecilia opened her mouth to politely decline, but Anthony beat her to the punch.

"I'm afraid, gentlemen, that Lady Cecilia has promised the first dance to me."

She fixed him with a venomous glare.

"Shall we?" he asked, tucking her arm through his and leading her away from the hungry pack of men.

She refused to look at him. "Please, do not make me dance. You cannot be so cruel."

He patted her hand. "No, I cannot. I thought we might

take a turn about the room instead." He felt her struggle to keep from limping as they strolled through the horde of guests. "Or," he said, his conscience getting the better of him. "We could find a place to sit."

She nodded curtly.

Keeping her arm firmly on his, he led her out of the ballroom and down a back hallway.

"Where are we going?" she demanded.

"Somewhere we can talk in private," he whispered.

She tried to pull away from him. "What could we possibly have to talk about?"

He gripped her hand and shoved her through the entrance to Whitford's library, shutting the door behind them. She forced a laugh and shot him a condescending glance. "Keen to reenact our first encounter, my lord?"

He pushed her down onto a chaise lounge so she could not complain that we was making her walk, and loomed over her. "Do not play coy with me, Cecilia."

She smirked, trailing the edge of her fan down his chest. "I never play coy."

He wrenched the fan out of her hand and tossed it away. "What do you plan to do about Captain Brinkley?"

"Nothing at all, my Lord," she demurred.

"Don't lie to me, Cecilia!" he shouted. She attempted to stand, but he pushed her back down. "You mean to kill him, don't you?" Her lip curled. "Don't you?" he pressed.

She looked up at him, a cruel smile forming at her mouth that did not reach her eyes. "Yes," she hissed.

"How? Poison in his champagne? A dagger in his back when he meets you for a tryst?" he demanded. "This is madness, Cecilia! You will get yourself found out!"

She stood and shoved him away from her. "How dare you presume to place value on my pain!" she shouted. "Do you know that when he first raped me, he gloated that he was taking a Duke's daughter's virginity? The only thing that stopped me from killing him at that very moment was the satisfying knowledge that he was two years too late for that." She bared her teeth like a cornered dog and Anthony checked the impulse to back away. "And every time after, I restrained myself from killing him because I knew I would be caught! They would have found me out and sent me home to prison, or put me in front of the firing squad before they ever learned I was a woman. And now, I have the opportunity to free myself and avenge myself, and you would hold me back? His death is nothing compared to what I have suffered! His life is my due!"

"And your life will be forfeit if you take his!" Anthony pinioned her wrists in his hands to keep her from leaving. "They will hang you at Tyburn. I will not see you die Cecilia! I will not!"

She wrenched herself free and grabbed him by the collar. He stumbled back against the bookcase, the unexpected show of strength knocking the wind out of him.

"Enough! Do you give me no credit, Anthony?" she asked. "I will not murder him! I will give him a death befitting his crimes and my honor."

He recovered his breath and the import of her words struck him. "You mean to challenge him to a duel?"

Her eyes sparked with vengeance. "Yes."

"And if he should kill you?"

"Unlikely. He is good, but I know his handicaps."

"But you are wounded!" he said, exasperated. She was determined to see harm to herself.

"Then he and I shall be evenly matched. And if he does kill me, which I do not predict, then I shall still be rid of him."

Anthony leaned back against the bookcase and ran his hands through his hair. "It is still madness, Cecilia," he said again, as if proving a madman's madness to him could cure him.

She frowned at him, shaking her head in disappointment. "It is something I must do. Please try to understand."

"Oh, I do understand. I don't like it, but I understand. That doesn't mean I won't try to stop you."

She glared at him.

"You're right. I won't be able to stop you."

She laced her satin gloved fingers through his and brought his hand up to her heart. "I would much rather have you as a friend then an enemy."

He lifted her hand to his mouth and kissed her knuckles. "I could never be your enemy. Nonetheless, it will not work."

She snatched her hand away. "Why? You doubt my ability with a sword?"

"No," he smiled ruefully. "Surprisingly I do not. But he will never accept your challenge. The moment you challenge him, he will reveal you to the world. He will not fight you. He does not respect you enough."

A shadow of fear sped across her face. She shook her head slowly. "He would not…" She looked down at her feet, frowning in frustration, then took his hands in hers again and fixed him with her honest, steady stare. He had the brief feeling that he should be worried before she said, "Then there is only one course to take. You must make the challenge."

"Me? I am not the best swordsman, Cecilia. I would happily die for you, but it would not set you free."

"No, you fool." She gave him a gentle slap to the shoulder. "You challenge him. I come as your second. Then I fight in your stead. He will not refuse me then, when the challenge is already made, and thus prove himself a coward."

Anthony considered saying no immediately. It was fool-hardy. It was dangerous. And it was the only honorable chance for Cecilia to have her revenge and free herself of Captain Brinkley. Every bit of his gentlemanly upbringing told him to say no. But Cecilia clearly didn't need a gentle-man. Thank God, as he wasn't one. Perhaps it was only her deep, begging amber eyes; perhaps it was something else, but he found himself saying, "Alright."

She let out a great sigh of relief and wrapped her arms around his neck, pulling him in for an embrace. For a moment, he wondered if she was using him again, drawing him in, playing on his lust...

At the moment, with her heart beating a contented refrain against his own, he could not care less.

"So what do we do?" he asked.

"I let him find me tonight. He told me he would. Then you find us, and you slap him in the face with your gloves."

He laughed at her ability to put such a serious topic in a humorous light. "And do you think he will take the challenge?"

"I believe so. He is the son of a peer, and though he has no honor in regards to women, he holds his family honor in high esteem. He will take the challenge, or he will be disgraced. I will see to that."

"Then, my Lady Vengeance, you should make your way back to the ball."

CHAPTER SEVENTEEN

Anthony's eyes never moved from Cecilia as she made her rounds in the ballroom, gracefully ignoring the censorious looks of the gossips and gently refusing the numerous men who entreated her for a dance. He watched as she brought a delicate hand to her forehead, feigning a headache as yet another gentleman requested the pleasure of her company on the dance floor. She smiled dazzlingly at the man and begged his forgiveness, and he gave it gladly, suggesting that he would be honored by a dance from her at the next ball she attended. Anthony frowned. He did not like this false side to her. It was simpering, normal, and all too boring. It was not the Cecilia he knew. He knew she was only playacting, but he found himself wishing she would throw convention to the wind and be herself in society. He wanted to see how the world would react to the real Lady Cecilia Warenne. Doubtless the world would be scandalized, more scandalized than it already was at her presence. But the nobles of Bath could use a healthy dose of scandal, and there was no one better equipped to thrust it on them then his Amazon.

Captain Brinkley found her too quickly for Anthony's taste. He made a curt bow before her and kissed her hand, then tucked her arm into his and requested the pleasure of a turn about the room. Cecilia threw Anthony a casual glance to be sure he'd note their departure, and went with him willingly. Brinkley's actions so closely mirrored Anthony's own earlier that Anthony found himself growling into his champagne. He watched them disappear into the hallway behind the ballroom and followed.

Cecilia had agreed to lead Captain Brinkley to the library for their assignation. Anthony crept up to the library door and pressed his ear against it. He had to wait to make his entrance until Brinkley had Cecilia in a compromising position. He gritted his teeth as he listened. He wanted to burst in on them now and break the Captain's neck. But he would do as Cecilia wished. He had been unable to do anything else since he'd made love to her. Who was he fooling? She'd been commanding his every action and thought since the moment he'd first laid eyes on her.

"How quaint of you to attempt to dissuade me from my purpose, Cecilia," Brinkley was saying. He heard Cecilia utter a small gasp of protest and forced himself to not think of where the man was touching her.

"Captain, I am a wealthy woman. I'm sure we could come to an understanding," Cecilia said.

"And I am a wealthy man. I like our current understanding."

"I could pay for a mistress for you."

"I don't want a mistress. I want you." Cecilia's next words were muffled. Brinkley must be forcing her into a kiss.

"Bend over." Brinkley's words were a merciless command.

"Please, Captain –" Her voice was tinged with pain.

Anthony burst through the doors, flushed with anger. Certainly this was as compromising a moment as any. His eyes flashed from the Captain, forcing Cecilia over a table, her hair grasped in his fingers, to Cecilia, her face screwed into a look of pure disgust. The Captain released her and she staggered to a chair, pressing her hand against her leg in pain.

"I beg your pardon," Captain Brinkley said, smoothing his jacket. "The lady and I were having a private discussion, if you wouldn't mind." He motioned Anthony towards the door.

Anthony forced his voice to stay icily polite, though he wanted to scream in Brinkley's self-satisfied face. "It appears the lady is not enjoying the discussion as much as you are."

Brinkley took a step towards Anthony, his brows knotted in irritation. "I don't know who you think you are –"

Anthony slapped him across the cheek, cutting his words short. Out of the corner of his eye, he thought he saw Cecilia give just a hint of a smile. "Your actions are unconscionable, Sir."

Brinkley massaged his jaw with one hand and fixed Anthony with a glare. "You insufferable –"

"You have offended the lady's honor, and for that you will pay." Anthony pulled himself up to his full height, gratified to see he trumped Brinkley by an inch. "Expect my formal challenge to you in the morning. Do not refuse me, or you will be proclaimed a coward." He held out his hand to Cecilia. "Lady Cecilia, shall we depart?"

Brinkley grabbed Cecilia's elbow as she stood. "You are not going anywhere."

Before he could check the impulse, Anthony's fist shot out and collided with Captain Brinkley's jaw. The man careened backwards and fell senseless against the table. Cecilia gasped.

"Do you think that was a bit harsh?" she asked. "He is a hot tempered man."

Anthony drew a shuddering breath, collecting his gentlemanly reserve, and took Cecilia's hand in his. "I thought you thought that nothing is too harsh for Captain Brinkley."

She smiled up at him triumphantly. "You were magnificent! You played the part to the hilt!"

"I assure you," Anthony said, wrapping his arms around her. "I was not acting at all."

Chapter Eighteen

T he formal letter of challenge Anthony sent to Captain
Brinkley's house in the morning read thus:

*My resolve is as firm today as it was last night. I will see
you bleed for your crimes against the honorable Lady.
Instruct your second to meet mine today at two 'o clock in
the back room of the King George's Cup to discuss terms.*

Your servant and your enemy,

— Anthony Maltravers, Viscount Stirling

Cecilia read the letter over his shoulder as he sat at the
writing desk in his study. "Very succinctly put," she said.

"It would be a waste of time and ink to spend more words
on him," Anthony retorted as he sealed the letter and handed
it to the waiting footman. The man bowed and left.

"And now we must weave the web of deception just a bit longer," she said, relaxing onto the settee.

"What do you mean?" he asked.

"On the day of the duel I will be your second," she explained. "But I can hardly show up at the King George's Cup today to meet *his* second. He would realize the ruse and refuse the duel."

"I see."

She smiled at him. "I'm afraid you must go yourself."

"And what do I say to explain that?"

"Explain that your second is indisposed. Knowing the company Lord Stirling keeps, Captain Brinkley will hardly be surprised." Her eyes sparkled with mischief.

"Are you calling my friends drunken sots?"

"Your words, not mine." They both laughed.

Anthony's brow furrowed. "I was wondering last night, as I was unable to sleep due to your naked form lying next to me in bed –" he chided her with a click of the tongue.

"I warned you," she snickered. "I always sleep in the nude."

"As I said, I was wondering, will he choose swords or pistols?"

She frowned, chewing her lip. "Is it true what you said last night? That you are not a particularly good swordsman? That was not merely false modesty?"

"Regrettably, yes."

"And is this common knowledge?"

"Amongst my friends, and at my club and my gymnasium, yes, it is well known that I am a better shot than I am a swordsman."

"Ah, good." She smiled, relieved. "Captain Brinkley is a thorough man. He will find this out. He will use the knowledge to what he thinks is his advantage. He will instruct his second to choose swords."

"And this is preferable to you?" He bit his lip to keep from expressing too much worry. Clearly, Cecilia thought herself an equal match for Captain Brinkley in a fair fight. Somehow, though, Anthony doubted the fight would be fair. After all, the Captain had no honor.

"Most decidedly, yes."

"Who will he choose as his second?"

"He has only one close friend in Bath just now, Lieutenant Lightman. Lightman's an honorable man. Second son of a peer, just like Brinkley. He'll probably choose him." She paused and made an impatient sigh. "Though I can't for the life of me think why Lightman allows himself to be friendly with Brinkley at all. He has much more honor regarding women. I know… well, George knew him. He came whoring with us a few times. He is ridiculously polite to women, even to prostitutes. He even once punched a fellow officer who slapped a prostitute's behind too hard." She laughed. "I'm sure he knows nothing of Brinkley's dealings with me, or he would not be his friend. Hopefully he will assume that my anger with the Captain is related to my brother, and not to myself. And if he suspects something, I doubt he would turn me in for killing Brinkley. He would assume my honor to be worth more than Brinkley's life."

"You assume a great deal," Anthony said quietly.

Cecilia shot him a puzzled look and frowned. "You have misgivings?"

He buried his face in his hands and shrugged. "How can I not? I think perhaps this is the most dangerous and foolhardy thing I've ever done."

"Foolhardy?" she asked, incredulous. "You think defending my honor is foolhardy?"

"No, not that. Just that I am helping you at all." He smiled up at her. "No one who knows my reputation would guess it in a million years."

"Well then," she said softly, limping over to him and sitting on his lap. "Your reputation is built on lies and those who know it know nothing of you. You are a rake, but that does not preclude you from having honor or empathy. Enjoying love making does not mean you forfeit your soul." She kissed him, brushing her breasts against his chest. "At least I hope it doesn't," she whispered. "I'd hate to think I am already damned."

He drew her into him for another kiss, parting her lips with his tongue, clutching her to him. She ran her hands through his hair and pulled his head back. Her lips brushed his Adam's apple, and he sucked in his breath, his heart pounding against his ribcage, deafening him.

"Promise me, if I die tomorrow, you will come find me in Hell," she said, her mouth tattooing every word into the skin of his throat.

He could not think it. He would not imagine it. "Cecilia," he began, but she silenced him with her lips over his. He held her to him, refusing to let her words steal this moment from him, until she pushed him gently away.

"I will see you tomorrow morning." She whispered in his ear, her voice calm and resigned. "And I will be ready."

"Yes," he finally managed to say, but she was already gone, and the fear slinking its way across his chest would not let him follow her.

CHAPTER NINETEEN

A young man, perhaps younger than Cecilia, seated himself opposite Anthony in the back room of the King George's Cup tavern at precisely two o'clock. He wore his regimental uniform with stiff pride.

"Afternoon," he nodded curtly. "You are Lord Stirling's second?"

"No," Anthony replied. "I am Lord Stirling."

The young man lifted his eyebrows in surprise.

"My second is indisposed at the moment," Anthony explained. "Had a bit of a long night." His words couldn't be closer to or further from the truth. Cecilia was injured, but she had fallen asleep the moment she'd taken her clothes off, and slept for at least nine hours. He hadn't had the heart to wake her, though his cock wished he had. Anthony only hoped that a good night's sleep would prepare her for the fight tomorrow.

"I see." The man seemed to accept the excuse. "Allow me to introduce myself. I am Lieutenant Lightman."

So Cecilia had been correct. Anthony shook the man's hand, perhaps more tightly than necessary. "A pleasure to make your acquaintance."

"Indeed. Shall we get down to business? I see no point in keeping up idle pleasantries."

"Naturally," Anthony answered coldly.

"Captain Brinkley prefers swords."

Cecilia had been correct again. "Tell the Captain that is acceptable to me."

"The time and place?"

"Six 'o clock tomorrow morning, Bellingham Park, behind the Oriental gardens."

Lieutenant Lightman nodded in assent. "And the terms? The Captain thought perhaps to the blood would suffice to satisfy the disagreement."

Anthony stared the young man down as he was sure Cecilia would have done. "I am afraid the Captain has misrepresented the disagreement to you, then. I demand to the death."

The young man frowned. "Are you certain, my lord?"

"The insult was his, so the terms must be mine. I demand his life." He clenched his hands into fists under the table, his fingernails digging little welts into his palms. For Cecilia's sake, he wanted desperately to acquiesce to 'to the blood,' but he knew it would not serve her purpose. She needed Brinkley dead. She wanted Brinkley dead. Frankly, so did he. He just didn't want Cecilia doing the killing…

Lieutenant Lightman considered for a moment, then nodded. "To the death, then." He stood and offered his hand to Anthony in a gesture of respect. "Good luck to you, my lord."

Anthony regarded the proffered hand coolly, then shook it. "I cannot say in good conscience that I wish Captain Brinkley the same."

The young man bowed. Anthony nodded. They parted company.

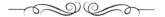

A breeze from the library's open bay windows swept through the room, relieving some of the stale odor. Fresh air. He set his wine glass on a table and moved to the balcony to clear his head. He stood in the doorway a moment, eyes adjusting to the darkness of the night sky, before he noticed that he was not alone. At the far end of the balcony, a statue stood. A thin Grecian dress trembled against the stone in the nocturnal draft, and he watched as it clung to the pert breasts, round buttocks, long poised legs. He reached out, caressed the figure's arm, traced the finely carved strands of hair flowing languidly down its back. He kissed the hard neck, cupped the unforgiving breasts. His thumb pressed against a dent in the smooth stone, and he looked down at the statue's torso, pale in the moonlight. On the left breast, just over the heart, was a small hole, the mark of a sword's point. He ran his fingers over the wound. A trickle of blood seeped out, ran down the statue's chest...

Anthony woke with a start, a cry of protest dying on his lips. Sweat dripped down his face and neck. He rubbed his eyes with the backs of his hands. Outside his window it was still dark. The grandfather clock in the hallway chimed four times. Two hours left to go. He forced his eyes shut but all he could see was the ooze of blood against marble skin.

He stood on shaky legs and rang for his valet.

CHAPTER TWENTY

Five-thirty. Cecilia stood on the steps of her house, waiting as Anthony's carriage pulled up. She was dressed in breeches, black leather Hessian boots, a man's white shirt, and a tan waistcoat. Her breasts were bound against her chest and her hair was plaited severely back. Anthony could see little of the elegant woman in her that had captivated him at their first meeting. She was cold, hard, unforgiving as stone. A regimental officer's sword hung against her leg. He shuddered involuntarily and rubbed his hands against her thighs. She wrapped her cloak around her shoulders and pulled the hood over her head.

Anthony opened the carriage door and she climbed inside, her gait even and determined. No limp. She looked at him from under her hood, her amber eyes concealed by shadow. He held his breath.

"Everything is arranged to our satisfaction?" she asked.

He nodded.

The carriage traveled in silence, cutting through the empty streets, wheels echoing against the paving stones like the footsteps of pall-bearers bringing a coffin to church. Anthony closed his eyes. *Ooze of blood against marble skin.* "Don't die," he whispered, the words a command.

The carriage turned into the park and followed the path to the Oriental gardens. "I won't," she answered, her words a promise.

The field in the rear of the gardens was empty. Early morning fog rolled over the ground and dew-covered blades of grass licked at their boots as they alighted from the coach. Cecilia drew her sword and made a few practice lunges, lightly favoring her left leg. Anthony watched the grace, the skill of her movements. She was quick and nimble, her footwork impeccable. She held her blade almost carelessly, the movements of her right arm seemingly effortless. She was a master. Much better than he. *Please God*, he thought, *make her better than Brinkley*. And then, for good measure, because he wasn't sure God would listen to him, he begged the Devil too.

A second coach pulled into the clearing and Captain Brinkley and Lieutenant Lightman stepped down, the requisite doctor following. Cecilia drew her hood further over her face and moved behind Anthony. Brinkley strode up to them, dragging the tip of his sword casually in the grass. He made a short bow to Anthony.

"Lord Stirling." The captain stripped off his jacket and threw it to Lightman. He smiled arrogantly. "Shall we get this over with?"

Anthony stepped aside and motioned to Cecilia. "By all means. I regret to inform you, though, that I am unable to fight this morning. Dreadful cold, you know." He coughed unconvincingly and gestured to Cecilia. "My second will be taking my place."

Captain Brinkley frowned, a glimmer of recognition flashing across his eyes. He stepped forward and pushed back Cecilia's hood. First he smiled, then he laughed. Lieutenant Lightman let out a small gasp. "Lady Cecilia." Brinkley made a mocking bow. "I should have guessed, of course."

"Captain Brinkley." Her words were crisp in the cold morning air. She tossed her cloak to the ground and took her beginning stance. Anthony watched as the muscles in her shoulders flexed, tensed.

Brinkley threw up his hands in exaggerated surrender. "My lady, you know I will not fight you."

"You will." She held her stance.

Lieutenant Lightman stuttered, "Th-this is hardly –"

Brinkley cut him off with a wave of the hand. "Cecilia, I will not fight you." He turned to walk away.

Cecilia reached behind her back and pulled a pistol out of her waistband. Anthony held his breath; his heart leaped once, then he was sure it stopped beating altogether. She leveled the gun at Brinkley's back and cocked it.

The noise made her opponent stop. He turned back to face her.

"You will fight me with honor, or you will die without it." She shrugged. "I have no preference." Her voice was low and menacing. Brinkley bristled and clenched his left hand into a fist. "Make your choice, Captain."

Brinkley's second spoke up. "Lady Cecilia, I hardly think your brother would wish you to put yourself in harm's way like this."

"Lieutenant Lightman," she answered impatiently, keeping her eyes focused on Brinkley, "for the friendship you showed my brother I will not kill you here and now, but I suggest you stay out of my way and hold your tongue, if you value it." The young man stepped back, intimidated by her tone. "Which death do you prefer?" She asked the Captain.

Brinkley nodded and saluted her with his sword. She tossed the pistol to the ground. Brinkley took advantage of the motion to lash out with his sword, but Cecilia ducked under his lunge and nicked him in the ribs, sidestepping teasingly. He growled and her lips smiled in return, though her eyes remained cold as stone. *Ooze of blood against marble skin.* Anthony gritted his teeth.

"Frigid bitch!" Brinkley spat. He beat back her blade.

She parried his attack. "Revenge is a dish best served cold."

Anthony forced himself to take a deep breath. Slowly, he bent and reached for the pistol, holding it concealed against his leg. His eyes never left Cecilia.

She was flawless, her footwork anticipating Brinkley's every strike. The bigger man lunged after her, his strength and anger far eclipsing hers. She kept her motions fast and relaxed, her face still as she focused entirely on avoiding the Captain's livid barrage.

Cecilia feinted to Brinkley's left and he parried, pushing back with his full force. She leaped back and he lunged forward again, his sword crashing into hers. He brought his knee up to her gut and punched her sword arm with his left hand. From somewhere behind him, Anthony could hear Lightman shout, "Fight fair, man!" but the words didn't register in his mind. He hefted the pistol in his hand, waiting for the right moment.

Staggering back, Cecilia lost her grip on her sword. It fell to the grass a few meters behind her and she lost her balance, falling with a thud into the wet grass. Brinkley rushed her and she scooted back on her bottom, but not fast enough. The point of his blade pressed against her left breast. He smiled down at her, his mouth a cruel incision in his face. He pushed his blade an inch further and she hissed in pain, a small dot of blood appearing on her shirt.

"Don't make me kill you, Cecilia," he murmured.

Her eyes held his gaze, but her hand slowly searched the grass behind her for the hilt of her sword. Brinkley clicked his tongue in admonishment. With a sharp merciless motion, he drew back and stabbed down towards her heart.

Anthony raised the pistol; the right moment had already passed. Cecilia caught the Captain's blade in her left hand. The fingers of her right hand reached her own sword and curled tightly around it. Anthony pulled back the hammer of the pistol with his thumb.

Blood pooled between Cecilia's fingers. She gritted her teeth. With a roar of frustration, Brinkley wrenched his blade from her grip. Her right arm sliced upwards; the tip of her sword slid smoothly into his abdomen. The Captain stood motionless for a moment, teeth bared in anger. Slowly, his blade slipped from his grip. His knees sagged. He looked down to the point where her sword mated with his body and grimaced in disgust.

"Bitch," he said, his voice barely above a whisper.

Cecilia thrust her blade further in. Brinkley choked, spitting blood on her. Wiping her face with her left sleeve, she brought her right leg up and kicked him in the groin. He toppled backwards, her sword sticking out of his belly just below his ribs. Her whole body shook with an exhausted sigh, and she slumped down into the grass.

Anthony watched her fall back, his vision blurry and unfocused, and realized there were tears in his eyes. He dropped the pistol and rushed to her. Her breathing was shallow and fast, the stain of blood spreading over her heart.

He tore open her shirt and pulled down the bindings over her breasts to find the wound. Her hand caught his.

"I'm alright. It's not deep." She opened her eyes. "Help me up."

He lifted her arm over his shoulder, holding her lacerated hand gently, and hauled her upright. Leaning against him, she let him lead her to the coach. Anthony closed his eyes for a moment. He took a deep breath and held her closer. *Ooze of blood against marble skin.* He released the breath and looked down at her. She exhaled through pursed lips, subduing her pain. She was warm and soft under his hands. She was alive.

The doctor rushed to the Captain's side, black bag at the ready though it was too late. Lightman stepped forward and removed Cecilia's sword from the Captain's body and handed it to her.

"I will not pretend to know what this was about," he said cautiously, "but you fought with honor, and Captain Brinkley did not." He made her a short bow of respect. "You are truly your brother's sister, ma'am. You honor him."

Cecilia nodded to him. "I know I do. See to your friend's corpse, Lieutenant." The young man turned away. "And," Cecilia added, "I hope I can trust you to hold your tongue."

He searched her assured stare for a moment, then said, "Yes, my lady."

Cecilia rested her head on Anthony's shoulder. He nestled his chin in her hair and kissed the top of her head. Warm, bleeding, but alive. "I'm taking you home for a proper meal and a hot bath," was all he could bring himself to say.

She let out a small laugh. "Emma is too old to haul that much water upstairs," she chided.

"No," he said. "I'm taking you to *my* house."

She looked up at him, amused. "And my reputation?"

"I thought you once told me you didn't care a fig for it."
He smiled.

She smiled back. "And you once told me you were no knight in shining armor."

"You would be right to pay heed to that," he said, helping her into the carriage. His lips curled up in a lusty smile. "I'm only taking you home because I don't want anyone else's hands touching you but mine."

She leaned back against the seat and closed her eyes. "Is that a promise?" she teased, running the toe of her boot up the inside of his calf.

"Very much so."

CHAPTER TWENTY-ONE

Anthony lifted Cecilia out of his carriage and carried her up the steps to his house. She relaxed into his arms and closed her eyes. The butler who opened the door gaped in shock at the sight of the bloody woman in his master's arms and struggled for words.

"Fill my bath, and bring hot towels and clean bandages," Anthony ordered.

"Yes, my lord," the butler stammered.

Anthony carried her up the stairs and laid her gently on the bed. He removed her boots, her breeches, unbuttoned her waistcoat, pulled her shirt over her head. She watched him disrobe her, a peculiar look in her amber eyes. When she lay naked except for the cloth wrapped around her chest and left thigh, she pulled him to her and locked her lips with his. The satiny warmth of her skin melted through his clothes, scorching him wherever she touched him. He broke the kiss and forced himself to take a deep breath, willing his passion to cool. She smiled up at him, the strange incomprehensible emotion still haunting her gaze, and traced the line of his jaw with her forefinger. Anthony lay down in the bed beside her and pulled her into his embrace, clutching her as close to his chest as the thin layers of his clothing and her bandages would allow.

"Cecilia," he whispered, just to hear himself say her name. The syllables were honey on his tongue, sweet and satisfying. He tried to place what he was feeling, examining his limited experience of emotions. There was something there that he could not name. It tightened his chest and prevented him from speaking. He tried to call it lust. Relief. Joy. Need. It would not respond to any of these names. He inhaled the scent of her sweat, salty and earthy and female. The feeling in his chest reacted with a contented stirring.

"What do we do now?" she asked softly.

The sounds of maids and footmen bustling to and from the bathroom just beyond his bedroom door had died down.

He knew that the "now" she meant was not the immediate "now," but he did not have a satisfactory answer for her, and his lips were unfit for any use other than kissing at the moment, so he carried her into the bathroom and helped her into the tub. She eased into the hot water and slowly unwrapped the bindings from around her chest. The tight fabric left red grooves in the skin of her breasts. Unable to merely sit by and watch her, Anthony stripped and sat down behind her in the bath, enfolding her tired body in his. He pulled the ribbon from her hair and separated the strands of her braid. She leaned back against his bare chest and sighed. He cupped a handful of water and splashed it over her left breast, washing the dried blood into the bathwater. Then he took her left hand in his and cleaned the cuts on her palm. She reached back and stroked his cheek.

He wrapped one arm around her chest and let the other glide leisurely down to her sex. She purred in satisfaction and shifted her hips against his hand. His fingers hovered over her hesitantly, unsure what he wanted from her or what she wanted from him. Watching her chest rise and fall with slow, heavy breaths, he almost hoped she had fallen asleep, that he could have a moment alone with his thoughts. She stirred against him and rested her hands on his knees.

"Thank you," she whispered. He looked down at her face, at the single tear making its way down her cheek.

"Don't cry." He wasn't sure if it was what he was supposed to say, but his mind couldn't form his other thoughts into words. Her weight against his chest, the warm expanse of her ribs as she drew breath, rendered him helpless again. Her hair, stirred by the movements of their arms in the water, brushed against him, tickling his collarbone. Breathing in time with her, he memorized each heightened sensation. A muscle in her back shifted against his pectorals. *Thank God*, he almost said aloud; *this is real. This is not a fantasy.* She was flesh and blood against his flesh and blood, as human as he. Not a statue. Not a corpse.

"I'm not crying," she said softly. "George is. He knows he is well and truly laid to rest now."

"And what about you?"

She paused for a moment, thinking. "I shall receive a letter in a few weeks informing me that George has given his life in battle. By Christmas, the Dukedom will pass to my father's second cousin."

"And will you be taken care of?"

"For the past few years, I, well George, has been completing all the necessary paperwork for all the ducal properties and funds, excepting the title and what is entailed, of course, to pass to Lady Cecilia Warenne at the event of George Warenne's death. I will be more than taken care of. I will be one of the richest women in England."

"Ah." His heart sank. So she did not need him. Doubtless she was now wealthier than he. He could make no offer to protect her financially. Considering she was a strong and stubborn female, he need not make an offer to protect her physically either. She would refuse it. There was nothing to tie her to him. She had gotten what she needed from him, and now the only way he could persuade her to stay by his side was to make love to her until she wanted no one else but him. And considering the way she'd chosen to give away her virginity, considering everything about her, that was unlikely to happen.

But, damn it all, he had not yet gotten what he needed from her. She had promised him what he needed in exchange for his help, and he could not shake off the feeling that she had not given him what he needed at all. She had given him her confidence, her secrets, her body. It was not enough. The unnamed feeling in his chest pushed him to say something, but his mouth, confused, would not open.

"And I should go home, soon. As soon as I am well," she continued. "Mother has continued the ruse of my confinement quite expertly. I would have been found out much sooner if not for her. I owe her much more than I can possibly give her, and she is all I have left." She leaned her head back against his shoulder and looked up into his eyes. She moved her hands up to cup her breasts. "I believe I owe you something as well," she whispered.

Anthony started to say, "You owe me nothing," but his body disagreed. He stood and lifted her out of the tub and carried her to the bedroom. She wrapped her arms around his neck, kissed his throat and the careless growth of golden stubble he had been too nervous to shave off that morning. He placed her on the bed and insinuated himself between her legs, pressing his chest into her breasts, anxious to feel her heat and softness, the beat of her heart against his. She arched her back up to him, her fingers digging into his shoulders. He ground his erection against her thigh, the wet fabric of her bandage chafing his groin. Moaning, she rocked her hips up against him, positioning the tip of his member against her wet opening.

No. Too soon. She had to want him more.

He edged back, raking his fingernails over her breasts, down her abdomen, trailing a line of impatient kisses down her belly as his hair dripped pearls of bath water onto her skin. His tongue found the pink bud in the cleft of her legs and laved it, slowly at first, teasingly, then more urgently as she gripped his hair between her fingers and bucked her hips up against him. *Make her want more.* She tasted of aching hunger, or perhaps that was only what he felt but he couldn't be sure. He buried his face in her sex, the strange tight feeling in his chest snaking around his heart, spurring him on. She cried out and dragged his head up to meet hers, claiming his lips, still wet with her arousal. As her tongue sought his, a wave of weakness wracked his body as he struggled to maintain control. He fell to his elbows over her, his arms unable to hold him up.

"Anthony," she said breathlessly into his mouth. "I need you inside of me."

The feeling in his chest recoiled, her words touching on his own selfishness. Need. He thought he'd felt it from the moment he'd laid eyes on her. He needed her. It was a possessive, despotic word. It demanded. And he could demand nothing from Cecilia; he simply could not. With her, all he could do was beg, take what she gave and nothing more. He… loved her too much.

What? No.

He did not feel love. He never had. He believed in pleasure in the place of love. Her words came back to him. *I did manage to confuse love and carnal pleasure rather badly.* And now she was confusing them again, with him. No, that was him. *He* was confusing them. The room spun. He couldn't think.

He found himself sliding off the bed, walking towards his dressing room. "I have to go," his voice said, and surely those were another man's words, not his.

"Anthony?" she asked, puzzled. "What did I say?"

He closed the door behind himself and shut her out.

Chapter Twenty-Two

"Father." Anthony looked up at the greying man sitting opposite him at the breakfast table. For the past few days, he had stalked through the halls of his father's house in angry silence. He had left Cecilia lying naked in his bed and ridden to his father's country estate, unsure of where to go or what to do to be rid of her. He needed time to let himself think. But he had not been rid of her for one moment. He felt her insistent, desperate caress in every movement of his clothing against his body. The autumn breeze through his hair when he went riding was her breath on his face as she whispered "I need you." Every classical statue in his father's garden called her poise to mind, drowning him with longing to relive their first meeting. Every night was plagued by fitful dreams of Cecilia's skin, red with blood. Cecilia's lips, open in a cry of pleasure. Cecilia's luscious hair, lapping against his chest in the bath. Cecilia's honest, trusting eyes. He slept naked, hugging the sheets to him as if they could in some small way replace her touch, her warmth. He woke every morning cold and miserable, with the same condemning thought gnawing at the corners of his mind. Need or love? Need or love? Need or love?

"Yes?" his father said.

Anthony swallowed. "I have been considering matrimony, Father."

His father looked back down at his morning paper and shrugged. "You know my requirements. Is she rich and titled?"

Anthony's lip curled in distaste. "She is the daughter of a duke. And she is rich as Croesus."

"Make an offer then, before someone else snatches her up." The Earl of Huntington took a bite of poached egg.

"That's just it, though," Anthony said, setting his fork down with much more force than necessary. "She's perfect. For you, that is. But I want to make sure she's perfect for me."

The Earl looked at his eldest son over the top of his paper and raised an eyebrow. "Don't be sentimental, Anthony."

Anthony continued, ignoring him. "It's been a week since the thought first crept into my mind that I might actually love her. And the moment I thought that, I ran away." His father raised another eyebrow. "And not for the reasons you think. Not because I didn't want to find myself wrapped around a woman's finger. I feel the greatest pleasure of my life when I'm with this woman. If this is what love feels like," he pounded a fist dramatically into his chest, "then I do not fear it at all.

"But every time I think of her, I think of you. Of your mercenary, though I will admit simple, criteria." The Earl frowned and opened his mouth in protest, but Anthony would not let him get a word in. "And I think, she is rich and she is titled. She is perfect. And then I think of you and mother, God rest her soul, and the cold, miserable existence you slogged through while you were married. And I think, it cannot be right to put love and familial obligation into the same thought. If what I feel is love, then it is warm and giving and all-forgiving, and it is nothing like what you had. Considering you and mother never seemed to love each other, *how* am I to judge my own love? I have nothing with which to compare it. Is it love I feel? Or is it a fierce but passing infatuation that, if saddled with matrimony, would sour like your own marriage and leave me miserable. And if you know me at all, you know that I am married to my own happiness. I could never put myself or a woman through what you put mother through. So I am left with the opinion that I cannot, in good conscience, consider the object of my affections and your own wishes at the same time. If I am to examine my emotions, I must forget everything you've instilled in me. It has been excessively difficult." He paused.

"What exactly are you saying?" his father asked, his voice hard.

Anthony took a deep breath and pressed his fists against the edge of the table. He focused on his father's cravat pin, rather than the man's stony glare. "Did you and mother ever love each other?"

The Earl snorted. "She was my wife. Of course not."

"Did you ever love anyone else?" Anthony asked. The Earl frowned. "Anyone?"

"I certainly didn't raise you to be this mawkish," Anthony's father sneered. "I can hardly recognize you as my son."

"How can you?" Anthony asked. "How can you be so cold and yet live?"

"Be careful what you say, Anthony," the Earl warned. Anthony did not heed the warning.

"I cannot uncover my own feelings until I have freed myself from yours, Father."

The Earl leaned back in his chair but said nothing.

"I am cutting myself off," Anthony said finally, his words quiet and certain.

"Think before you act."

"I am cutting myself off. I do not want your allowance. I do not want your opinions. I do not want your ridiculous ultimatums about my future wife. I want to think for myself. I want to be in love." *I want someone to love me.*

"You need my money," the Earl admonished.

"I won enough money at the faro tables last month against Lord Darling alone to set me up modestly for the next year. And should the woman I love return my affections as I am sure she does, provided I have not irrevocably insulted her by my abrupt departure the last time we were together, then my pride is not so great that I would not allow her to support me, considering how fabulously wealthy she is and how much she would enjoy having me at her mercy. In fact, I have learned in the past fortnight that feeling dependent on a woman is not an unpleasant feeling at all, provided the woman on which one is dependent is..."

... is Cecilia Warenne.

The Earl huffed in disgust and set his paper carefully on the breakfast table. "You are a fool, Anthony."

"Well, that decides it then, doesn't it? Didn't someone once say men are all fools in love? So I must be in love," Anthony proclaimed, and a satisfactory shade of red overcame his father's face.

"I have put up with your ungentlemanly behavior and waste of money for nearly thirty years, Anthony," The Earl spat. "If you continue to treat my fatherly affection with such distaste I shall have no qualms in seeing that all you ever get from me is my title upon my death. Not even a penny with which to burnish it."

"That was the idea," Anthony smirked. The further he pushed, the more certain he felt. That must mean he was either heading for a monumental fall, or he was doing the right thing.

"You will regret this."

"I regret not staying in Bath in the arms of the woman I love and sending you a letter to this effect rather than coming here."

"If you give up your inheritance, I shall give every last cent to your brothers."

"And no doubt they will drink and gamble it away as I have for the past nine and twenty years," Anthony said and rose from the table. "Goodbye father, and wish me happiness, if you can find it in your egotistical heart to do so." He made a curt bow and walked out.

CHAPTER TWENTY-THREE

She was beautiful; a vision in pale green, her hair pulled into a severe bun, one errant curl cascading down over her shoulder. She laughed at something the gentleman beside her said, and tapped the tip of her white lace fan against his chest reprovingly.

Anthony stood, frozen, the crush of guests pushing past him into the ballroom. It had been nearly a week since he'd seen her, two days since he'd decided he couldn't live another day without her beside him. He felt as if he was seeing her for the first time. No mystery, no intrigue, just the sheer relief that she hadn't somehow vanished from his life as she had so many times in his dreams. She was a feast for starved eyes, and he drank in every graceful motion, every politely false smile, every word formed by her soft kissable lips, every shift of her weight as she favored her left leg. She looked every inch the demure daughter of a Duke. Except for her amber eyes. He watched them as she smiled up at the throng of men around her. She noted their surreptitious stares at her cleavage with bored impatience, giggled absentmindedly at their jokes. She was sad. He could see it. As he approached, he selfishly prayed the sadness was over him.

Because he loved her, every fascinating and unladylike inch of her, and if she didn't love him, if she didn't miss him as much as he'd missed her, he would…

In the words of Shakespeare, he would do a desperate outrage to himself. Dear Lord, but the thought of this woman had the ability to call to mind more of his long-forgotten education than his tutors had ever hoped he'd retain.

"I think I understand now what you meant," he whispered into her ear. The gentlemen around her backed away in shock at the impropriety of the gesture.

She started at the sound of his voice and turned slowly to face him. He held her gaze and the effort pained him to the bone. She was angry. Hurt. She masked none of it, letting her silence speak for her.

He offered her his arm. "Are you dancing tonight, Lady Cecilia?"

She snapped quickly back into the veneer of calm disinterest, nodding politely and resting her hand on his. "Only the waltzes. I am not quite recovered enough for anything more vigorous."

Only the waltzes. How inappropriately scandalous. How refreshingly Cecilia. "This waltz has already begun. May I claim – may I *beg* what is left of it?"

She frowned, puzzled at his choice of words. He longed to kiss her, show her what he meant with his body, rather than his words. She might awake his mind, but his mouth was still slow to show it.

"Yes," she said.

He led her to the dance floor and held her close. She smelled of lavender. "You've changed your perfume."

She smiled slightly and looked away. "What you mean is that I've finally had the time to buy some. I am not using men's soap anymore."

"Quite," he chuckled. He began again. "I think I know what you meant when you said you would give me what I needed."

She looked up at him, hopeful. "Do you?"

Anthony took a deep breath and looked down at her bosom, at the tiny pink scar just over her heart. The wound had healed quickly, on the outside at least. "You did not mean sex."

She smiled sheepishly. "I did, a bit. Just a little bit."

He held back a laugh and continued. "You gave me something to love, which was not something I ever thought I needed," he whispered. "Or wanted. Or thought remotely possible." He smiled. "You gave me a purpose."

She looked up at him and he could see the words catch uncertainly in her throat. A single tear formed in the corner of her eye. "Yet you left," she said quietly.

He wanted to wipe away the tear, but he didn't dare let go of her for a single moment, certain she would run from him as he had run from her. "Forgive me?" he begged. "It is a long, long crawl up from Hell. I have been trying very hard."

She blinked and shook her head for a moment, then fixed him with her demanding stare again. "Perhaps," she said, the devilish smile tugging at the corners of her mouth, "you would like a companion for the journey?"

He frowned in mock confusion. "You mean someone with whom to practice monogamy? How shocking." He clicked his tongue.

"How shocking indeed," she murmured.

"I shall lose all my friends."

She smiled. "If they are anything like you, they shall come around when they see me riding astride."

"You wouldn't!"

She laughed, low and contented. "I have lived too long a man to change my habits now."

"You will embarrass me constantly, won't you?" he teased.

"I shall endeavor to enjoy my life. I daresay the ton will find that exceedingly embarrassing."

He held his breath and asked the question he'd wanted to ask for days. "Will you be my companion?"

She frowned. "Are you asking me to marry you? Are you sure?"

He grinned mischievously. "I must warn you, I have given up my father's money and will someday be left with an Earldom for which I have not the funds for upkeep. I will be a leach upon your purse strings for the rest of your days."

"Mmmm," she mused, biting her lip. "It sounds like a lot of trouble."

"Indeed." Anthony held her close and hoped she felt the beating of his heart, fast and determined, through his jacket. There were too many layers of clothing in the way, but surely she could feel it, when it beat louder than the music.

Cecilia smiled her wicked smile. "I like trouble."

(Not quite) the end.

Cecilia and Anthony's adventures are not yet over…

OTHER ROMANCES BY M. BONNEAU

Aphrodite, Undressed (Regency Romance)

The four orphaned Hunt siblings are alone in London. Daphne, the eldest, is willing to do almost anything to keep them out of the poorhouse, and London's reigning rake is happy to help… for a price.

Too Cool For School (Contemporary Romance)

A high school history teacher falls hard for one of his rebellious new students… who is actually an undercover cop.

Light Me Up: Cyanide Rock Star Romance Book 1 (Contemporary Romance)

Chase has everything a sexy rock star could want, except for his band's gorgeous lighting designer, who doesn't take his flirtation seriously.

Rock My World: Cyanide Rock Star Romance Book 2 (Contemporary Romance)

When a broken-hearted rock star and a cold-hearted MMA fighter come together for one wild night, they find all the passion and healing they could ever ask for.

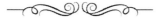

Rhythm and Blues: Cyanide Rock Star Romance Book 3 (Contemporary Romance)

Buffy is in love with his bandmate, Nikki. Nikki is in love with her bandmate, Buffy. It's a shame neither of them knows it.

ABOUT THE AUTHOR

M. Bonneau has been a writer since before she could write (at the age of four, she was staying up past her bedtime dictating stories and poems to her mother). M always dreamed of being an author and earned her BFA in Creative Writing (with minors in music and history) from Chapman University in Southern California, where she was part of the Tabula Poetica Reading Series and edited the journal Sapere Aude. She worked as a nanny after college where, in her free time, she read her first romance novel. She was inspired by the many romance authors writing strong, flawed, feminist heroines, and decided she wanted to do the same. "Statue in the Moonlight" was her debut romance. She now teaches drama and creative writing at a Montessori junior/senior high school and writes romance, fantasy, and poetry in her spare time. You can find her online:

Website:
mbonneau.com

TikTok: @blueskiesblacksoul
Twitter: @mbonneauwriter

Made in the USA
Middletown, DE
05 December 2022

17179224R00080